With my
Best Wishes

Out of This World

from

Graham

for

2010.

Out Of This World

By

Wingerworth Wordsmiths

This edition first published in England in 2009 by
Wingerworth Wordsmiths
www.read-us.com
E-mail: wordsmiths@live.co.uk

ISBN: 978-0-9564044-0-4

This edition designed and typeset by Marie O'Regan
Cover Art © 2009 Marrion Carding

Printed by ASR Tradeprint, 515 Abbeydale Road, Sheffield, S7 1FU
Bound by FSP, Unit 1, 104 Fitzwalter Road, Sheffield, S2 2SP

British Library Cataloguing in Publication Data.
A catalogue record for this book is available from the British Library.

Contents

There are many reasons why novelists write, but they all have one thing in common – a need to create an alternative world.
John Fowles, *The Sunday Times Magazine* (1977)

Preface

About Us

Wingerworth Wordsmiths are based on the outskirts of Chesterfield on the edge of the Peak District. Currently there are 12 members in our writing group, several of whom are published authors in their own right, and we meet weekly to read and discuss ongoing work and receive essential feedback. In addition we attend other literary events and invite guest speakers to come and share their experiences with us. Among the highlights this year was an excellent workshop with Derbyshire Poet Laureate, River Wolton. We have also been invited to participate in the *Winter Warmers* performance at the Pomegranate Theatre in Chesterfield in December, an invitation we were delighted to accept. By far the most exciting development though was the decision to enter for the David St. John Thomas Anthology Prize. Since it was our first attempt this was unknown territory, but every member of the group contributed time and effort to the project, and the resulting book was something we were all proud of. Even so, we little thought that it would win. When it did we were absolutely elated. It was a wonderful experience to be able to send a team to the Society of Authors in London and receive the trophy and winners' cheque. Perhaps more importantly though was the moral boost that each member of our group received from that success, and the increased confidence we have gained as a result. No-one can put a price on that. The book eventually sold 300 copies and raised several hundred pounds for local charities.

As always, we attribute much of our success to the unstinting support and guidance of our tutor and mentor, Paul Bamford.

About this book.

This year we offer *Out Of This World*, a new and purpose-written collection of short stories and poems to which everyone has contributed. The title is also the central theme which provides necessary cohesion to the whole. It was reached by consensus after some keen debate. We felt it offered real scope for everyone. As anticipated, interpretations of the theme vary greatly, encompassing genres as diverse as science fiction, crime, the supernatural, historical writing and humour. Based on the edge of the Peak District we are privileged to be in a location that is also out of this world, an idea reflected by the poetry contained in this book. We hope that everyone will find something to enjoy, and that this anthology will prove to be an entertaining and thought-provoking read.

Our aim this time is to sell 500 copies and thus raise more money for our chosen charities. They are Ashgate Hospice in Chesterfield; and the Chesterfield branches of the Parkinson's Disease Society and the MS Society. Proceeds from the sale of the book will go to these causes. They were chosen because they have particular and personal significance for the members of our group.

Finally, but by no means least, we would like to thank Marie O'Regan, our typesetter and page designer, for her excellent work on the layout of this book. We also extend heartfelt thanks to Clive Jaques and his staff at A&R Tradeprint in Sheffield. Following our appeal on BBC Radio Sheffield last May, they have lent their support to the project and have most generously printed this anthology free of charge.

Jane Croft 2009.

Accidental Hero

By
Colyn Broom

'Help! Come quickly!'

With the aid of his acute super-hearing ability, Wonderman's ears picked up the panicked voice and he immediately sprang into action, running down the nearest deserted alley and into a concealed doorway halfway along.

After a moment, a figure emerged from the shadows. He peeped up and down the narrow passage before moving into the light. As he did so, his bright red and yellow, one-piece, figure-hugging stretch lycra suit, glistened in the late afternoon sun. On his head he wore a similar-coloured half-balaclava mask, which covered most of his head and upper face, leaving just his mouth and nose exposed; on his chest was a large yellow "W".

Good, no one was around.

Starting to sprint in the direction of the scream, he smiled to himself. There was no person on the planet that could run as fast. It was part of the gift with which he had been blessed, after arriving thirty years earlier. His parents had been marooned on Earth after making an unscheduled stop – following a meteorite storm, which had disabled their space ship.

They had traded him, with a childless couple who lived on a farm, for some old tractor parts and a hair dryer, which they had used to repair the "Four-inline, Self-centring, Epicycle train, of Flux-cored Ion-capacitor Relays, used in the Gravitational Warp Signature field, by the Interstellar, Radian Molecule, Photon Conversion chamber" – in the engine.

He had no complaints. They had been the most wonderful Mother and Father that anyone could have wished for – and very understanding. Even after burning down two-thirds of the farm buildings once, while practicing his "Heat-Ray Eye Beam" thing that he had stumbled across, barbecuing several of the livestock in the process. On the plus side though, he could mow the lawns faster than anyone in the county.

As he ran through the busy streets, he heard the voice again shouting for help. He knew he had to find its owner; it was his job. Following the cry, he came upon a large ethnic woman who was being mugged by two youths in their mid-twenties. They had somehow managed to force her head between some railings, where she was clearly stuck, while they rifled through her belongings. Wonderman stopped, seeming to appear from nowhere, and startled the pair of attackers.

'Stop what you are doing, or there will be – trouble,' he announced. The two youths glanced at him, laughing as they continued with their quest.

Wonderman held up his right hand, palm facing them, preparing to use his "Reverse Magnetic, pushing force field, energy thing". (He had discovered this unique talent quite by accident after holding up his hand to catch a bus and, upon boarding, finding all the passengers squashed up at the front of the vehicle in a heap, along with the driver).

The two assailants were abruptly thrown backwards, one of them bouncing into the trapped woman, who let out a horrific cry of pain.

'Whoever you are,' she screamed. 'Please don't help me anymore; I don't think I'll live through it!'

'Sorry madam.' Wonderman winced. 'I'll have you out in a jiffy.'

Focusing his eyes on the imprisoning metalwork around each side of the woman's neck, he once again used the power of his "Heat-Ray Eye Beam thing," cutting through the railings as if they were made of putty. As the steel melted and gave way, the large woman lurched backwards, squealing and clutching her throat.

'You've burnt my bloody neck now – look at it!' She removed her hands revealing two long, red blisters, one down each side. 'Why don't you throw me in the canal while you're at it, just to finish me off?' Picking up her handbag, she swung several times at Wonderman, each connecting with surprising accuracy. 'I tripped…'

Thwack!

'…*And* fell…'

Crunch!

'…Through the railings.'

Smack!

'These two lads…' she continued, pointing at the stunned prostrate bodies, '…were searching for some butter in my shopping bag to rub around my neck…' She swung and hit him again with a dull thud. 'Should I have them arrested and sent to the electric chair…?'

'Oops, time to leave,' mumbled Wonderman as he took another well-placed swipe from the hardest handbag he'd ever known.

With a single bound, the shiny red and yellow suited hero, leaped over the two recovering youths and up onto the rooftops, then out of sight. *Can't get it right every time,* he thought, his body still stinging from the barrage.

Down below, the angry woman helped the two stunned lads to their feet, unaware of the hot piece of metal from the railings, nestling snugly within the lining of her coat. Steady whips of smoke rose unnoticed into the air. As Wonderman left the scene, he smiled with the satisfaction of knowing that he had helped save another innocent member of the public from herself.

Calling to be Found
By
Sue Pacey

Illy had grown to love this forest long ago. Perhaps it was just as well.

Today, the clearing beneath the tall elm trees provided dappled shade. The early summer sun fought its way through spreading branches, casting shafts of light on the glade below. The effect was like something from one of his childhood storybooks. Midges danced in the tracks of light as they speared their way to the ground, dusty and indistinct; the promise of another warm day ahead.

Another endless day in this secret place where few ventured.

Grandfather had first shown Illy this clearing when he had been little more than five. The man had placed a finger to his wrinkled old lips and smiled down at the child.

"Go quietly, my boy. This is a place of magic and you must not disturb the elves that live here. One day, if you are very quiet, you may see them and they will dance for you." He bent down to the child's level in conspiracy, beckoning him closer. "But, mark my words, you have to be silent. Only then will the elves dance."

And, when the time came, Illy had been silent. But the elves had not come to dance, or anything else for that matter.

"It was a lie! Grandfather...Help me!"

The plea went unanswered, as always.

The leaves of last autumn still lay beneath the trees, remaining where they had fallen to be buried by the winter snow. But now, from the russet carpet, came fresh green shoots, striving upward in the search for light and warmth. They would have to work a little harder this year, but then, Nature loves a challenge.

Illy knew that, as the years went by, the forest floor would surely rise, burying her secrets deeper and deeper.

A twig cracked softly. He looked on as a young fawn stepped tentatively into the clearing searching for food. For a moment it halted, sniffing the air, tasting the signals borne on the breeze; its head raised and alert. So close to his hiding place was the creature, that he could almost have reached out and touched it. Then, with a sudden start, it was gone.

It seemed such a long time since the first flakes of winter's snow had fallen. Within the day, the glade had been covered by a thick, protective blanket of white. And, with it, all hope was gone until the next spring when perhaps, people would come again.

***

The girl was laughing loudly as she ran into the clearing, her chestnut-coloured hair in flight behind her. Her cheeks were glowing rosy-pink with the chase. Looking around quickly for a hiding place, she fled behind the tall elm. Flattening her back against its trunk, she breathed hard, trying not to giggle.

"Krystina...where are you?"

The young man ran into the clearing. "I'm coming to get you, Krystina. It's no good running!" He began to search, laughing all the while.

So, running was no good. How Illy wished he had run, instead of choosing silence.

Oh...if only he had run.

With a whoop of delight, the young man found the girl, sweeping her off her feet, to carry her high in the air. He spun her around, safe in his arms. They fell to the soft earth beneath the tree, her arms encircling his neck. Her green eyes gazed into his as he kissed her tenderly.

Illy watched, silently...secretly from his hiding place.

How like Leila she was. The same green eyes, the same gaze; the way they lit her face when she looked at her lover...the same eyes that had looked at him.

He wondered what the young couple would have done if they had known he was watching, so close by. But, there was no fear of discovery. He would not call. He had stopped calling of late...these past few years.

Perhaps if he had only run... He wondered if Leila had run and not, like him, stood in silent, insolent vigil. If she had run, then at least they would have shot her quickly; cleanly. He could not bear to think what might have happened to her if she had not run. He had heard the stories. It was too terrible to contemplate! The taking of his Leila.

As he had been taken with the others, when the Serbs came.

All the men and boys together, marched from the village to the forest. Nico had been afraid, clinging to his older brother's arm for protection. Illy had been afraid too, sensing the fate of them all. And, when the shots came, he held Nico close so he would not see. In his hand he clutched the watch that Grandfather has given him when he turned eighteen; the watch that had the inscription – *To Illy Malovich:a fine grandson.* Still holding his trembling brother, they fell together into the freshly dug earth.

One day, he knew they would come, the men with dogs...to search for the lost, the forgotten... the nameless; one day, when men had learned to stop hating.

When they found him, they would also find clutched in his hand, the watch bearing his name and the younger boy's head resting on his shoulder.

Then, the world would finally know and the elves would dance once more.

Out Of This World
By
Jane Croft

A clawed hand round the scruff of his neck thrust ten-year old Kevin into his bedroom. Then he heard his gran's strident tones.

'You'll stay in there until your parents get home, you little blighter.'

For a moment she glared at him from the threshold, red-rimmed eyes burning in the cracked desert of her face around which locks of grey hair writhed like angry snakes. Then the door slammed and locked and he was alone.

Grimacing, he pulled off his eye-patch and the black scarf that covered his spiky red hair and flung them aside. Then he threw himself on the bed and reflected bitterly on the injustice of his imprisonment. It had only been a game after all. Pirates always made their prisoners walk the plank. The pond wasn't even that deep. As for the Koi carp, his dad had been ripped off there; they definitely tasted muddy when cooked. Plus, the flames of the camp fire had barely touched the shed.

Through the open window drifted the sounds of children's laughter and splashing water from the neighbours' pool. Sunlight splintered on the glass, accentuating his cruel predicament. Moving past the toys and books lining the shelves of his room, his brooding gaze came to rest on the computer game above the desk: *Mission to the Labyrinth of Death.* The hard-muscled, armour-clad, blaster-wielding figure of his hero, Colonel Dare, stared out of the cover at him. The rugged face expressed concern. Kevin sighed.

'What now, Colonel?' he asked.

'You have to get out of there, Kev,' replied the familiar voice. A moment later, Colonel Dare leapt out of the troll-infested labyrinth and landed on the desk.

'But how?' asked Kevin. 'The door's locked. Besides, the evil sorceress lurks in her grotto at the bottom of the tower. You know what capture means.'

Dare nodded. 'Interrogation, starvation rations and probable torture.'

'The guard dogs would give me away in any case.'

'Ah, yes, the venomous Yorkies. Small but deadly.' Dare looked thoughtful. 'That leaves only one choice, Kev.'

'You don't mean...'

'Yes, the window.'

Kevin gulped. 'It's an awful long way from the ground, Colonel.'

'That's why it's not barred. The sorceress thinks no-one would dare attempt to escape from the Fortress of Doom that way.'

'But how will I do it?'

'Use the sheets of course.'

Kevin wondered why he hadn't thought of that himself. Having dragged them off the bed, he knotted them together and tied one end to the wooden frame before throwing the rest from the window. He watched it snake away down the wall. To his intense disappointment the bottom end reached only as far as the flat roof of the kitchen below.

'Never mind,' said Dare. 'We'll have to improvise.' He pointed to a metal coat hanger on the back of the door. 'We must take that.' As Kevin retrieved it he added, 'Bend it in half.'

'What's it for?'

'You'll see. Now, are you ready?'

Kevin nodded. He shoved the bent hanger in his pocket and climbed on to the sill. Heart pounding he grasped the sheet and swung out over the void. Dare jumped on to his shoulder and they began their descent, reaching the flat roof with ease. From the kitchen below came strains of eerie music.

'Jurassic FM,' said Dare. 'The sorceress listens to it when she's concocting her vile potions. With luck she'll be too busy to notice our escape.'

They looked around for the guard dogs but they were conspicuous by their absence. Dare grinned.

'All clear, Kev. Let's get off this roof. Only be sure you don't touch the man-eating bushes or the radio-active grass.'

'But we're surrounded. How can we avoid them, Colonel?'

'With the aid of the coat hanger and that cable.'

'The washing line?'

'That's what the sorceress wants you to think, Kev. It's really a cunningly- disguised, titanium-reinforced, hyper-glide wire.'

'How does it work?'

'Sit on the edge of the roof. That's it. Now put the coat hanger over the line and take firm hold of both ends. Got it?'

'Yep.'

'Good. Now... jump!'

As he leapt he heard the Colonel's familiar battle cry. 'Yeeeehaw!'

Seconds later Kevin was whizzing down the garden at eye-watering speed. Then he heard Dare's voice in his ear.

'Booby trap, Kev! Look out!'

Too late he saw it. Plastic pegs shot in all directions as he ripped through the coloured wash. Wet fabric clung to his face. Half blinded he hurtled on, unaware of the looming poly-tunnel, crashing through it in a shower of compost and green tomatoes. His velocity barely decreased, slamming him into the boundary fence beyond. The ancient wooden panel shattered as he was catapulted into the neighbouring garden where he hit the padded side of the prefabricated swimming pool. Through a semi daze he heard screams and an ominous creaking sound as the side of the pool began to buckle.

'Tidal wave!' cried Dare.

Out of this World

Kevin's blue eyes widened. He tried to stand but a wall of water lifted him off his feet and swept him and the pool's three occupants down the lawn like tumbled stones. Gasping and choking they were washed up on a patio. Kevin staggered to his feet. The garden around him had been transformed into a shallow lake in which stood islands of vegetation. A misshapen pile of blue plastic indicated the remains of the swimming pool. Beyond it, the ribs of the poly-tunnel leaned at drunken angles against the ruined fence.

'Bummer, Kev,' said Colonel Dare.

There followed shouts and expletives and the sound of hurrying feet. Then he heard the shrill voice of the sorceress.

'Kevin!'

His freckled face paled. 'We'd better get out of here.'

'Good idea,' replied Colonel Dare.

Together they made a dash for the adjoining garden fence. Kevin grabbed the top of a post and vaulted, desperation lending him added momentum. He was in midair when he saw the vast terrace of newly-laid, wet concrete below.

Endless Shade
By
Leonie Martin

The lights of mighty London shine,
Tall thrones for sharp suits scrape the sky,
You rose from reach of powers divine
And robed in silken shirts and ties
A virtual empire swiftly built,
In glass topped lifts you glide from guilt.

We helped you build those ivory towers
With calloused hands, hard graft and sweat
While you were banking bonus hours
The likes of me sank steeped in debt,
As chaps chewed business over lunch,
Our nation bit the credit crunch.

Smooth dealers hedged our homes away
You boomed at us to spend and spend
With plastic promises to pay
And toxic debts stacked end to end;
The Emperor's new clothes were found,
And now, I'm sleeping on the ground.

My grafter's hands hang, stained with grime,
Though not ground in through gainful work,
No more those honest hours will chime,
Around my box, dark shadows lurk
Above my head, march well-heeled feet
Beneath my blanket, lies the street.

The sewers of London creep and bleed,
My once-proud soul now sunken low,
Pale victim of the years of greed
And robed in rotten rags of woe
Beside the river Styx I'll stay
In endless shade; your dues to pay.

Special Places
By
Sue Pacey

I sat in a high meadow where the earth meets with the sky,
On a winter's day, fog swirling all around.
If I ever longed for paradise it is right here in this place
That was butterflies and daisy-covered ground.
And in that lovely meadow on a morning damp with dew
By a pretty rowan tree in early bud
I sat in contemplation of the hand that gave it all
Making shades of green no human ever could.
On a chill October day with leaves blowing round my feet
I am watching Nature's cycle on the wane
Warmed by special inner peace that enfolds me when I'm here
In the promised hope that spring will come again.
In the snows of January, bare trees stark against the sky
I saw a hunting vixen slinking past
If I ever long for solitude, I will find it in this place
Where I'm part of the enchantment Nature cast.
Seasons all may come and go but the plan remains the same
In that perfect place where earth meets with the sky
Where I can be alone with something beautiful- at peace
To rest and dream and watch the world go by.

Flashback Fair
By
Rosie Gilligan

It's all so familiar: thudding generators; the cacophony of a hundred pop songs; multicoloured lights carving ellipses and circles in the night sky; and the stink of fried onions and candyfloss.

I come to a stop, and am immediately taken back to when I was barely a teenager, lying on the sand next to the Pleasure Beach, and wishing I could afford the entrance fee. I remember how I fell asleep and dreamed I was a small child, whizzing at tremendous speed on a carousel, held by my father on a wooden galloping horse. We rose and fell against a backdrop of blurred sounds, colours, until I woke up to find my brother kicking sand in my face.

'Well, are we going in then, Christina?'

My friend, Lorna, is waiting impatiently. I'm standing in front of the entrance to Flashback Fair. 'I wonder how it got that curious name,' I say.

'When I was little, I asked my granddad about that,' she says. 'He said he'd asked his granddad the same question. And he didn't know either.' She grabs me by the arm and pulls me along.

We wander between the booths, stopping to watch the punters roll pennies, or lasso small objects, with ineffectual hooks. At the rifle range there's a man shooting at pock-marked metal ducks. They follow one another in a dignified single file, on the wall behind the greasy-haired attendant.

'That reminds me of when I was little,' says Lorna. 'My dad shot three ducks in a row and won me a huge teddy bear. I was *so* thrilled I insisted on carrying it home. But it was too big for me and I tripped and fell – and sprained my wrist. Dad took me to hospital and, while we were waiting to be seen, he told me a story.'

'Go on, then,' I say, looking at her with feigned interest.

'*Well*', she says, smiling and blushing slightly, and clearly pleased to have the opportunity to tell the tale, 'he said, when he was a boy, he went to the zoo and held a real live bear cub. But it was too much for him to handle, and it bit his hand. *He* ended up in hospital too.'

'That's spooky,' I say, but I've heard this tale before. Lorna forgets what she's already told me. For some reason, she doesn't bother to relate that her father had to stay in hospital for a week, during which time the doctors discovered he had a tin farmyard animal stuck up inside his nose. His mother had recalled looking for it years earlier, without success.

We move to the food stalls and stand, mesmerized, by the candyfloss machine.

'I don't care how often I see this, it *still* fascinates me,' says Lorna.

We watch the assistant move the stick around the bowl, and see the pink cotton wool bundle grow, as if by magic. A girl wearing a pink shell suit and pink hair ribbons reaches up eagerly to grasp it. We move away towards the rides.

'I wonder when funfairs stop being about just having a good time, and start being all about *memories* of having a good time,' Lorna says.

I'm impressed by this philosophical turn. 'I suppose it's when we stop going on the rides, and start watching others take them.'

She nods. 'Ok, so let's go on the Big Dipper, then create a memory for the future.' She grabs my hand and pulls me towards the ticket booth.

When I was younger, I used to leap on the Dipper without batting an eyelid, but today I'm shaking all over as we strap ourselves into the battered blue and red car. Before I have the chance to escape we're chugging relentlessly to the top of the ride. I know what's coming. Now I hate that sickening, petrifying, stomach-lifting sensation as we hurtle down and round and upside down, before stopping and stepping out, all wobbly and bewildered.

Well, that was last year. And now here we are again at Flashback Fair.

'Do you remember going on the Big Dipper?' says Lorna.

'As if I could forget,' I say. 'So, what shall we ride on this time?'

Golden Leaves
By
Carol Vardy

The wind howled through the trees.
The birds huddled in the hedgerow.
The autumn leaves, golden brown,
Came fluttering, cascading, all around.
The wind blew them hither and thither.
They crackled under foot.
The acorns bounced
When they hit the ground.
The squirrels picked them up.

The Alien
By
Carol Vardy

'Hey, stop that,' Tom snarled out of the corner of his mouth, as the blond haired boy was about to pinch him. 'I'm an alien from outer space so you'd better go, Earthling, or I'll beam you up into my space ship.'

The boy's mouth dropped open and he scurried away as Tom leant forward as though to grab him. The shopping mall was particularly busy that day and his patience was waning. He smirked to himself as he heard the child speaking to a young woman.

'Aunty Lynn, that green alien's after me.'

Lynn grabbed Rob's hand and mumbled, 'Yes dear.'

Her mind was on other things. She gave a sigh and pushed strands of fair hair off her face. Her jeans and tee shirt hung loose on her slight frame. She'd lost a lot of weight since her sister and husband's accident. Three months had passed and it hadn't got any easier.

Rob wasn't the only kid to poke and prod Tom. When he took this temporary job he hadn't expected to be wearing a lime green suit. He thought he would be standing behind a counter, displaying a new green drink. Instead he looked like a big, fat, rotund blob. On the helmet were two antennae with bulging eyes that flashed as

24

they bobbed up and down. The adults laughed at him, the kids weren't too sure, but he'd put up with the prodding and poking because he started his new job on Monday.

Lynn woke early and, after a quick coffee, she began making sandwiches. Today was Amy's twelfth birthday. A party had been arranged in Sherwood Forest. Amy's brother Rob couldn't wait; he wanted to play at being Robin Hood. Lynn's mind drifted to her sister Rosie and brother-in-law, Tony. She'd told them they could always rely on her, not realising how hard it would be. Her thoughts were interrupted as Amy entered the kitchen, her blonde hair tousled, her eyes full of sleep, but with a big smile on her pretty face which was flushed with excitement.

'Happy birthday darling,' said Lynn and passed Amy a parcel wrapped in colourful paper with a huge silver bow on the top.

Amy glanced at the gift tag and then quietly tore off the paper.

'Thank you,' she whispered, lifting out a portable CD player. She gave Lynn a big hug and tears fell down her young face.

Lynn squeezed her tight and whispered, 'I know darling, I know. Come and help me, it's your party today.' She was trying to sound happy for Amy's sake.

'Thank goodness that's over,' muttered Tom, making his way to the staff car park. 'I don't want to see any more kids. I'm ready for a long cool lager.'

He couldn't be bothered to get changed; he'd give them a laugh at the pub. With great difficulty he managed to squeeze his large green bulk into the car, his antennae bent double. Good thing there was a slit to see and breathe through, he thought.

Lynn parked the car on the roadside. Amy and Rob helped to carry the cool boxes to the picnic area. They covered the tables with red tablecloths and arranged the food. They'd just finished when Amy's friends and their mothers arrived. Screams of laughter filled the air as they played.

'Lynn, can you smell smoke?' asked one of the mothers.

The Alien

She sniffed the air, looked around. In the distance, clearly visible, were clouds of grey smoke. The other adults hastily began to gather the children together. As they ran they shouted for Lynn to hurry because there was no reception on their mobiles.

Cracking and popping sounds from the fire were getting louder. The sweet smell of the spruce trees was now replaced with the strong, acrid, smell of smoke. Where were Rob and his friend, Jack?

Amy dragged her hands through her hair and screeched; 'Rob! Jack! Where are you? Come quickly! There's a fire!'

Taking the shorter cut home through the forest, Tom sang along with the radio. He was starting to feel too hot and decided he really ought to pull over and nip behind a tree so he could get changed. Even as he made up his mind women and children suddenly ran from the woodland in front of him. He slammed the brakes on hard. They stared at him for a moment then jumped into cars and drove off at high speed.

Tom laughed and muttered, 'And that's before I take this suit off.'

His nose twitched and through the open windows he caught a strong smell of smoke. Some fool must have dropped a fag. It wouldn't take long to start a forest fire. He thought he heard a woman shouting and screaming. Prising himself out of the car, he tottered in the direction of the voice. A woman and young girl waved frantically and called to him.

'Quick, help! The children are missing!'

She was so agitated she didn't appear to have noticed his outfit. Amy clung on to Lynn. The three of them ran towards the clearing, their hands clasped over their faces, as the smoke grew thicker.

Rob and Jack were standing in the nearby glade, screaming. Tom grabbed hold of Rob but the boy tried to shake his hand off, his eyes wide and staring.

'I know you, you're that alien from the shopping mall.'

'It's okay. I'm not going to hurt you. I'm Tom'.

Lynn was running so fast he found it difficult to keep up. As they sprinted out of the forest, cars stopped as their drivers watched the spectacle.

Tom heard a voice shout, 'Did you see that? An alien! Quick, where's my camera?'

Lynn's car spluttered but it wouldn't start. Tom shouted for them to jump into his. At the side of the car he struggled out of the green suit, stripping down to his boxer shorts. Lynn blinked and couldn't help but smile. Amy and Rob giggled; they really had thought he was an alien. Not wanting to hang about he started the car and put his foot down. The green suit fell in a crumpled heap at the side of the road. As the helmet hit the road, the antennae bobbed up and down and the eyes flashed.

An article and photographs in the local paper reported the sighting of a vivid green alien with flashing eyes. It had rescued a woman and three children from a forest fire. Later the alien discarded its skin and revealed its true colours. At first Tom thought it most embarrassing, but then laughed. He supposed it had looked quite funny.

On Monday morning he showered, put on his new suit, and arrived at the car show- room punctually at 8.30am. A young salesman showed him to the office. He explained how, following the tragic deaths of the owner and his wife, her sister had been helping out with the business. Tom noticed a young woman at the filing cabinet and realised it was the same one he'd helped in the forest.

He gave a loud cough. 'Excuse me.'

She turned and then smiled. 'Hello, what are you doing here? Are you the new manager?' She eyed him up and down. 'You're not in your green suit.'

Seeing the salesman looking puzzled, Lynn and Tom laughed. 'Don't ask,' they said.

Out of this World
By
Claire Walker

The Royal Oak is starting to fill up on Friday evening. The setting sun shines through the windows, and the familiar smell of draught beer hits the nostrils of the regulars. In the corner, three friends, Bob, Dave and Geoff, sit in their usual seats.

'My round.' Bob stands and walks to the bar.

Dave swirls the dregs of his beer around in his glass before taking a swig. Wiping his mouth with the back of his hand, he nudges Geoff, and gestures towards Bob who orders their drinks at the bar.

'I bumped into Maureen outside the bank yesterday. Shame about her and Bob splitting up, isn't it?'

'Aye.' Geoff nods. 'Twenty-six years is a long time.'

'She weren't alone … she was with her new bloke … he looked very young.'

Geoff finishes the dregs from his pint. 'You said anything to Bob?'

'Nah. He'll find out soon enough.'

'Aye.'

'Do you know if he took that woman out that he met in here last week?'

'Aye. Took her to that fancy restaurant on the High Street.'

Both men nod, then look up at the television. It is showing the snooker.

Bob returns to the table, gingerly balancing three pints.

'Cheers, mate,' Dave says. He waits for Bob to sit down, then asks, 'How did the ... er ... date go?'

'It were ... well ... it were *different*,' Bob says, removing his tie and stuffing it into his Waitrose carrier bag. It falls onto the prawn sandwich that will be his evening meal. He looks at the television where the current player is set for a maximum 147-break.

The three men watch in silence, groaning when the player misses a shot.

'Shame,' Dave mutters.

'Aye,' Geoff agrees.

A chair is pulled out at their table, and the three men nod at their friend, Derek, who joins them. The four men sit in silence, eyes peeled on the snooker.

'All right, Bob?' Derek asks.

Bob nods; he is used to being singled out with this question of late.

'How's work?' Derek asks.

Bob is also used to people avoiding questions about Maureen, choosing instead to ask him about his job.

'Same old thing. Company is making redundancies, *I* do their dirty work for 'em.'

'Credit crunch?' Dave asks.

'Yeah. Seen it all before, though, haven't we?'

'Aye,' says Geoff.

'Bad at your place, then?' Derek enquires.

'Very. They fax a list of names through every week. I just check to see mine isn't on it.'

The three men laugh uneasily, before taking long swigs from their warm ale.

The snooker holds their attention for a while, until Dave breaks the silence. 'So, you were telling us about your date ... ?'

'*What* date?' Derek's eyes divert from the television.

'Bob met up with that woman from last week,' Dave clarifies.

'Oh ... er ... the one selling the raffle tickets?'

'Aye,' Geoff confirms.

All three men look at Bob.

He puts his pint down, and begins, 'Well … I think I smoked some marijuana.'

A silence falls around the table. Derek and Dave's mouths fall open, and Geoff cannot even muster a mandatory 'aye'.

Karen, the barmaid approaches their table with her tray of empty glasses. 'Evening gentlemen.' The four men mumble gestures. Karen tilts her head and addresses Bob. 'How are you, love?'

'Bearing up.'

'Must be hard.' She throws him a sympathetic look, then asks softly, 'Will you get to see the kids much?'

'Our Paula is 23, she lives in London. David's 25, lives local.'

The other men stifle a giggle as they divert their eyes back to the snooker.

'Right,' Karen says, 'They grow up so fast, don't they?'

'Aye,' Geoff answers for Bob, while placing his empty glass on the tray.

The four men watch Karen move onto the next table, before turning back to Bob.

Dave whispers, 'So, what did you mean by saying you *thought* you smoked *it*?'

Colour flushes to Bob's cheeks. He takes a sip from his pint, then explains, 'After the meal, we went back to her place *for a smoke*.' He makes speech marks with his fingers for the last three words. 'Her suggestion.'

No-one so much as blinks or mutters a word; they wait for Bob to elaborate.

'I'd never tried it before, so I couldn't ask what it was and … you know … look like an idiot.'

'Wouldn't know myself,' Dave mutters.

'Me neither.' Derek adds. 'What about you, Geoff?'

Geoff shakes his head into his pint.

Clapping is heard from the television, and the men turn their heads and watch the post mortem of the game in silence.

The pub doors are flung open and a group of young men fall

in under a cloud of testosterone and expensive aftershave. One of them is Dave's son.

Dave and his friends are temporarily distracted from the television, as they watch the youngsters.

Dave stands. 'Right, it's my round, and my young 'un's here. He'll want a drink.'

He joins his son's friends at the bar. 'All right, lads.'

'All right, Dad.' Dave's son stares over to where his father's friends sit in the corner, their eyes still peeled on the television.

'Looks riveting in your corner, Dad. No wonder you've come to see us.' The young men laugh mockingly. One chirps up with, 'What sad boring lives you all lead.'

Dave puts his hands deep into his pockets, and says, 'I can't tell you different, son.' He pulls out a twenty pound note and hands it to him. He orders more drinks and takes them back to his friends. They sit in comfortable silence.

After a while, Dave turns to Bob, and says, 'So, what were it like ... you know?'

All three men once more prize their eyes from the television to stare at Bob.

'It were ... it were out of this world.'

'Seeing her again, then?' Dave asks.

Bob is about to answer, but instead points to Geoff for his reply.

Geoff looks initially confused, then smirks as the penny drops. 'Aye,' he answers.

The four men chuckle quietly, before turning their heads back to the television.

The Fallen Angels
By
Gaynor Lynn Taylor

Angelica Starkey's sharp intake of breath caught the back of her throat. A small strangulated murmur penetrated the still darkness of the attic. The large bright star had moved erratically across the sky before plummeting to earth. She clasped her hand to her mouth as the bespangled object landed in the forest beyond the wheat fields, splattering into a million tiny sparkles that danced among the conifers before being extinguished.

'Did you see that Lucy?' she whispered to the sagging outline of her rag doll propped on the sill. 'I ought to wake father, the forest and fields are his, but I'm not going to. This will be our secret. I wish I had angels' wings.'

Father called her his 'Angel.' But from pictures she had seen, the only similarity was her mass of golden curls. His overprotective zeal was her constraint of liberty.

'Nobody else in the house could have seen it,' she told her silent friend. 'No other window is high enough to see over the tops of the farm buildings.' In the middle of the night Angelica often escaped the bedroom that she shared with her two brothers, and climbed the unstable, rickety steps.

The grandfather clock in the hall downstairs struck two; its sonorous chimes reverberating in every nook and cranny. Daniel and Peter had long since finished their crude jokes and raucous

32

laughter, trying to outdo each other under the feather quilt with their vulgar sounds and smells. Peter had climbed out of bed earlier, half asleep, as he did every night. The familiar pungent odour rose into the air as his warm urine hissed against the side of the chamber-pot, and splashed over the fluted edge. Angelica longed to have her own room. The boys were never made to say their prayers; never sought protection for themselves, the farm or anybody else.

She jumped from stool that gave her extra height; her bare feet and elfin frame made no sound on the boarded floor. She grabbed the doll by the arm. 'Do you know Lucy; mother says we all have a guardian angel to help us if we ask.'

Kneeling down and resting her elbows on the round wooden seat, she placed her hands together. 'Dear guardian angel, please help the star that fell to ground; keep the trees safe and please let me to go there one day.'

The winter snows of Ontario had come and gone six times since that night. It was a spring morning when Angelica noticed the blood-red stains. Fear struck a blow to her body. She was unprepared even though she knew something like this would happen one day. Her mother was comforting.

'It's quite normal, love, don't worry. You've become a woman.'

But what did 'becoming a woman' actually mean? Presumably she could now have babies, but she had no precise idea how that happened in humans, although she had observed the animals.

In the same week, father secured the attic and the room was finally hers. Each night she lit the oil lamp and piled up books on her bed. The biggest and heaviest was her grandfather's illustrated bible which she read a little each day. But she also borrowed text books from her teacher on biology, botany, English, French, science, history and geography. There was a selection of novels too, and stories from Greek legends.

One day she finished the dawn chores, milking the cows and feeding the hens, and strolled back to the kitchen with fresh eggs for breakfast. Her mother was leaning over the table clutching her stomach in pain. Angelica rushed to her side.

'What's the matter mother? Are you ill? Can I help?'

'It's nothing, just a bit of stomach cramp. It'll pass soon.'

Angelica examined her mother's pallor. 'You're working too hard mother. Allow me to help you more, please.'

Her mother pursed her lips. 'All right, from now on you can fetch provisions and deliver the eggs. Drive the buckboard to town this morning. There are things I need. Take Max. He'll protect you.' The sheepdog stretched out his front legs and wagged his tail. 'Do you remember when Peter pretended to attack you and Max grabbed his arm? Peter yelped like a cat.'

Angelica did remember, but her interpretation of Peter's attack was different from that of her mother.

Max loped alongside, occasionally diving in and out of hedgerows with a burst of enthusiastic curiosity. The prairie was covered with a burgeoning green haze. Angelica sang as they travelled. The blinding white reflection of sun was dispersing even the deeper snow drifts. Within a week or two, summer would arrive.

She sometimes accompanied father to town when he came to do deals with buyers from cities on the east coast, and several people waved to her. She pulled up the horse and climbed down. It was Peter's voice she heard. 'Well, well, if it's not our precious little angelic sister. I hope father knows she's here all alone.'

The light was behind her brother so she could not see his face. His sleeveless jerkin revealed well-developed muscles in his upper arms that glistened with sweat. He stood next to a young man shorter and stockier than him, but even more powerfully built. The two of them swaggered across the road to where she stood.

'What are you doing here?' said Peter.

'I've come for some provisions.'

'This is Billy.' Peter smirked as he inclined his head. 'Billy, this is father's *Angel...*'

Angelica smiled, but the appraising stare that she received from her brother's friend made her uncomfortable, as though he already knew what she looked like inside and out. She glanced down, unable to meet his eyes that devoured her like a trophy ready to be possessed. Instinctively, she lifted the scarf from round her neck and covered her long hair that glowed in the sunlight. Was this what being a woman felt like? She hurried inside the store.

When she came out, laden with brown paper bags, it was Daniel who was waiting for her. He was now 18, more than two years older than Peter. Angelica decided that the local girls would find him handsome with his dark hair, gleaming white teeth and gentle manner.

'Let me carry those,' he said. 'Peter told me you were here.'

'How come both of you are in town?'

'I'll tell you, if you promise to say nothing at home.'

'Of course I won't.'

'There's a war on in Europe, a big one involving many different countries. "The war to end all wars," they're saying, and as Canadians we've been asked to help. I'm here to sign up. I should be leaving next month.'

Horror seeped into Angelica's bones, her mouth fell open. 'Don't do that. Father can't manage without you.'

'I've thought long and hard. It's my duty. Father could sell the farm now and ease up some.'

'It's his life.'

'He still has Peter'

'Does Peter know?'

'Yes, he's jealous. He can't go because he's too young. But his reason for wanting to go is wrong. For him, it's a means of getting away.'

Angelica sighed. 'I suppose even Jesus had to leave home.'

Daniel grinned. 'He'd understand me then.'

The ride home *should* have been a delight. The air rushed through Angelica's hair and the sun warmed her face; yet her thoughts were preoccupied. Father would be hurt and angry by Daniel's decision.

There was a well-trodden path through the forest which shortened the journey by two miles. She turned off the road. The wheels sank into soft ruts and each hoof flung a divot into the air, miring the underside of the wagon. Without warning, Max ran off and disappeared. Angelica shouted to him to come back. When he did not respond she had no choice but to follow.

The horse snorted and began tearing up the sparse grazing as soon as she tied his reins to a low branch. Fronds of thick dead bracken and creepers caught against her ankles and shins. Branches of evergreens stung her face as she pushed past. This was now unfamiliar territory and she lost track of time. Max was barking but she could not see him.

She reached a thick hedge. Was that Max snuffling on the other side? There was a small gap near the ground, almost completely overgrown. She crawled on her hands and knees through the passage until she came to a clearing. Then she saw him. A shot of adrenalin flowed through her limbs, her pulse quickened. A few yards away stood the tall upright imposing figure of an Indian. She would have turned back except that Max sat at his feet. When the stranger lifted his hand, the dog flopped down and put his head on his paws with a gentle whine. Angelica was intrigued. The man wore a hide tunic belted at the waist, over an undershirt and leggings. He had moccasins on his feet. A necklace made of white bones and fancy beadwork adorned his chest. A single feather stuck out of the back of his braided black hair that framed a tanned, strong, angular face with high cheek bones, deep-set eyes and a long nose.

The Indian spoke first. 'This is a fine animal.'

'He likes you,' said Angelica.

The man smiled. 'All animals sense my being.'

She did not understand but was too polite to say so. Her eyes widened as she gazed around. Acres of land in the middle of the forest bloomed with a vast array of herbs, flowers, plants, grasses, bushes, trees and mushrooms. The heady combined aromas of spicy and floral scents both elated and calmed her spirits.

'What do you think of my garden?' asked the man.

'It's amazing.'

'I'd like to show it to you. I've waited a long time for you to come.'

His comment was unfathomable; yet she could think of nothing better. The specimens had come from all over the world:

China, India, South America, Africa, Japan and Turkey. She knew where these places were from her studies.

'But how did they come to be here?' she asked. 'Were the seeds blown on the wind or brought by foreign birds?'

'Probably!' the Indian replied. He smiled. 'Come Angel, there's more.'

'How do you know my name?'

'I do not need to know. I merely have to look at you.'

They walked together through another bower of firs to a place where a fire was lit and several small wooden shacks were built in a circle. Plants were in differing stages of preparation. Herbs, flower heads and stems were drying or being distilled for their essence and mixed with oil; roots were simmering and leaves being strained like tea. Coloured powders, ground by pestles, filled mortars and jars. Some had been bound already by a sticky honey-like substance and cut by a mechanical device into the shape of circular pills.

Angelica gasped in delight. 'You must have a lot of helpers.'

'As you see,' replied the Indian.

Actually she did not see at all, which was puzzling, but Max was totally at ease so she found it hard to feel threatened.

'Would you like to learn about my plants?'

'I certainly would.'

'Then please come again. I teach those who would hear.'

'What's your name?'

'My name is Eluwilussit from the Chippewa tribe.

'That's a long name.'

'Then please call me Eli.'

Angelica eagerly absorbed knowledge of anatomy and the causes of sickness and imbalances in the body. She carefully recorded the processing of medicinal herbs for cures of any kind of ailment. She told Eli about her anxiety for her mother's health since the doctor had now diagnosed cancer. He took Burdock root and Sheep Sorrel, Turkey rhubarb indigenous to Tibet and the bark of Slippery Elm. The formula and method was precise. He had made his decoction in an enamel pot and steeped it for several hours. 'Give the tea to

The Fallen Angels

your mother every day,' he said, 'it will detoxify the blood and curb the growth of the tumour.'

When Mrs Johnson, who ran the draper's shop in town, developed asthma, she was delighted to find she could breathe more easily after using one of the herbal treatments. 'What's in it?' she asked one afternoon when Angelica delivered her a package.

'A mixture of Aconitum, Lobelia, Cuprum . . .'

'Oh, enough, enough!' said Mrs Johnson. 'It's so confusing. I really don't how you remember it. All I know is that it's doing me the world of good.'

As she waved goodbye, Angelica saw Billy. He did not speak to her, just leered; she ignored him. She stopped to see Eli on her way home, and left her bicycle beside the path. But when she entered the clearing there was no sign of him.

'So this is where you hide away.' Angelica swung round. It was Billy.

He caught her left wrist and pulled her towards him. His mouth pressed against hers and she tasted his foul breath. He roughly squeezed her nubile breast and she scratched his cheek with her nails. He snarled, grabbed her by the shoulders and threw her to the ground, pinning her legs apart with his own weight. An acute pain seared through her shins. He lifted her skirt. She tried to scream; a fleshy hand covered her mouth. His fist punched her face with force measured to make her compliant but still aware. He released his grip; undid his flies. At his first thrust her insides felt torn apart. Had he cut her open? Her soul cried out. *Please guardian angel, help me; help me!* Before he had time to repeat the action, a log came down heavily on his head. He rolled over onto the ground, groaning.

The violent trembling of Angelica's lips made it difficult to feel the cup from which Eli urged her to drink. He helped her to sit up. Seeing Billy lying nearby, recollection flooded back and froze her mind. 'Will I have a baby, Eli?' Her voice was barely audible.

'No my child, you will not.'

But Angelica knew enough to understand that she was damaged and that nothing would ever be the same. She was no

38

longer pure but sullied. She felt like a fallen angel.

Billy recovered but was stunned. He stood up, disorientated and rubbed his head. 'You bitch! How did you manage to do that? You wait, I'll be back. Next time I won't be alone. There'll be nothing left of this place, or you, by the time I've finished.'

Angelica could not recall how she got home. But neither her mother nor father seemed to notice any change in her. Perhaps her dishonour could be hidden from them. It was then she saw the telegram on the table:

We deeply regret STOP Daniel Starkey STOP Killed in action STOP.

Eli's medicine helped mother to recover from her illness, but father fell into a deep depression, and when Peter left, he hired a manager called Jed to run the farm. They never saw Peter again, although there was no news of his death.

It was three months later that Billy came for his revenge. He arrived with a gang of nine young thugs carrying knives and bludgeons, weapons to be used against garden tools. Nevertheless, Angelica stood in the centre of the large clearing wielding a pitchfork. She no longer cared for herself, but if they damaged the plants she would kill at least one of them. Billy stood in front of his gang prepared for an easy fight. His head jerked; he took a step backwards, his mouth was a gaping rictus of fear.

'I'm not tackling that,' said one of the lads, 'I'm off.'

'Me too,' said another. They all turned and ran, pushing each other from behind in their urgency to retreat.

Angelica turned to Eli. 'What was all that about?'

Eli smiled. 'I guess they changed their minds.'

She stuck her fork in the ground. 'I was looking forward to a fight. I hate him. I shall never be able to wash away my shame.'

'Bitterness will destroy you. You must try to forgive, child.'

'Never,' she said shaking her head. 'I will never, never forgive.'

Jed was ten years older than Angelica. In the years that followed, the farm prospered under his leadership. Father agreed to try one of his daughter's concoctions and after a while took fresh interest. Angelica found herself gazing at Jed's face more frequently than she wanted to admit to herself. She liked his lopsided smile, the way his mouth moved when he spoke, the glint of fun in his eyes when he teased her, the way he pushed his hair away from his forehead, and frowned when perplexed. But he was a man. No God-fearing man would be interested in her, if they knew the dark secret in her heart.

She continued to learn from Eli. Then one day he sat down on a log opposite her. 'It's time for me to go, Angelica. My work here is ended. I can teach you nothing more. The rest you will learn from life.'

'But what shall I do without you?' she asked.

'It will be shown to you quite soon.'

Angelica threw her arms round him. 'Please don't go.' He hugged her. As she watched him stride away, his corporeal being seemed to fade and vanish. She wept.

Later that evening she sat on the veranda. Jed left the cowshed and strolled towards her. 'May I join you?'

'Please do.'

'You seem despondent, unhappy. Can I help?'

Perhaps it was the kindness of his voice but soon she was sobbing into his shoulder.

'You know that I want to cure sick people with my herbs?'

'I certainly do. Your fame has spread over half the province.'

'Well, I've been taught all I know by an Indian and now he's gone. He's been part of my life for so long. I miss him.'

Jed handed her a kerchief. 'I thought you learned these things from a book; I didn't realize someone was teaching you. What's his name?'

'Eluwilussit.'

'That's an old Algonquin word meaning "Holy One."'

Angelica blew her nose. 'That's strange. How do you know?'

'Promise not to tell?'

She remembered Daniel had once asked for the same vow. 'I won't tell.'

'My great grandmother was Cherokee. There are many who wouldn't associate with me, even now.' He paused. 'Can I make a suggestion?' Jed waited for her to nod her head. 'We have fields on the farm where you could propagate your herbs and plants. It would be closer than gathering them from the forest. I can give you a hand to move and replant them.'

Angelica beamed. 'Oh Jed, that would be wonderful!'

They spent months selecting plants, building new sheds and buying more equipment. A store was established in town. The venture injected new life into the family.

'Why not turn our surname round and call the business Key Star Remedies?' suggested father.

'Good idea,' said mother. 'I'd love to run the shop. Perhaps we can open in other places.'

Jed and Angelica sat most evenings on the terrace discussing their days. 'You have some wonderful products,' he said.

Angelica sighed. 'But they'll never be totally accepted without the approval of the medical profession.' She stood, and leaned back against the balustrade. 'I've made up my mind. I must study to be a doctor to gain credibility; then perhaps a university will test and approve them.'

Jed looked up. 'Some man will claim the discoveries for himself. You ought to retain patents on the production at least.'

'Whatever happens, we'll always know the truth,' she said.

Jed studied her face, rose to his feet and moved next to her. 'Angelica, do you know that . . . that I love you?'

She turned to look at him. 'Do you?'

'Is it possible you could feel the same one day?'

Angelica shook her head so that curls escaped their fastenings and fell onto her shoulders. 'I can never love or marry.'

'Why not? I don't understand.'

She noticed the tinge of desperation in his voice and her eyes filled with tears. 'I can't tell you. Please don't mention it again.

Can we be friends?'

Stepping back, he looked down. 'Forever,' he said.

Angelica caught sight of her reflection in the glass doors of the head office of Key Star Pharmaceuticals; a trim looking woman in a calf-length fitted red suit with a jaunty black hat, clutch bag and high-heeled shoes. She pulled on her gloves.

'Your car is outside, Doctor Starkey,' said the receptionist.

Angelica breathed in the cool air, grateful for her life. She asked the chauffeur to wait and walked across the main road to a large grey-stoned church. A man sat in the back pew, his crutches rested beside him; the top of one trouser leg was sewn together. A fit of coughing interrupted his prayers; he hawked and spat phlegm into a dirty grey rag.

The man looked up; recognition dawned. He tried to rise and shouted, 'Angelica, Angelica, please don't walk away. I prayed we might meet here one day.'

Angelica observed him in detail, swallowing hard to stop a sudden flood of repulsion and nauseous bile. Yet common humanity compelled her to approach.

'Billy,' she said in disbelief, 'Billy, is that *you*? What happened?'

'The war . . . gas. Been over twelve years now,' Billy explained. 'But I couldn't die until I made my peace with you.' He paused, biting his lip. 'I should tell you, your brother Peter is dead, stabbed by a rival drug gang. He died in my arms.'

Angelica could not speak, realizing how much she had loved the brother she always thought she despised.

Billy continued, head bowed, 'I sinned against you more than I can bear. You were angelic. My gross act turned you into a fallen angel. Can you ever forgive me?'

Angelica studied the altar's crucifix, supported by two celestial winged creatures. She slipped onto the seat beside him feeling light-headed, warm; free. An oppressive burden had lifted. 'Do I *look* like a fallen angel, Billy? Yes, I forgive you.'

Billy sobbed. 'Thank you. I'm so sorry for wanting to destroy what you loved.'

Her eyes lacked focus; she was standing amidst the herbs, clutching a pitchfork. 'Why didn't you?'

'I'm surprised you even have to ask. We couldn't compete with all those Indian tribesmen. There were hundreds of them aiming tomahawks or bows and arrows directly at us. It's a wonder they didn't trample your plants into the ground. Who were they?'

Her eyes glistened. She remembered the star that plummeted to the ground, spreading its sparkles across the trees. She paused and smiled. 'Those Indians Billy - they were fallen angels.'

The car followed the road to the family farm where Jed now managed the Key Star factories and plantations. As they drew up, she saw him packing suitcases into the back of his Ford Model 'A' Roadster.

'Where are you going?' she asked.

He stepped towards her. 'I can't stay here any longer, Angelica. You know how I feel about you, but you have a new life now.'

'Jed, my life is nothing without you.'

'Then marry me.'

Her voice wavered; was hesitant. 'There's something you ought to know. I was raped as a young girl. My heart has been full of hatred.' She looked directly at him. 'But God has helped me forgive the man who did it, and I've forgiven myself. Can *you* forgive too?'

Jed rocked her in his arms. 'Why didn't you tell me? You weren't to blame. It's in the past. What matters is our future.'

Angelica touched his cheek. 'It's taken me a long time to understand that. You're a good man Jed Harris.'

'So, is that a yes?'

'On one condition, if we have a son, we call him Eli.'

Entrapment
By
Sue Pacey

The mirror doesn't lie, Jennie. It can't. It's an object, incapable of rational thought, only reflecting what you see. The image that comes back is the true one; trapped within the silvered glass for ever.

Maybe it has a memory, Jennie, just like you. And you *do* remember, don't you?

The past is trapped inside your head. Perhaps it is the same with this mirror.

Do you remember the treats, Jennie – for being good? Daddy's special little girl?

Chocolate! The taste so dreamy. Such a lot of chocolate; white and dark. Just like your thoughts, Jennie. Now, put the memories back in the box where they belong, there's a good girl. Inside your head. Until the next time...until the *next* bar of chocolate.

Trapped forever, Jennie. You knew you would never leave home, even when you were old enough. Daddy's special, beautiful girl. A kind of 'parent trap', with chocolate-flavoured nightmares.

The girl in the mirror smiled in response to Jennie's own gesture, reaching out her hands...fingers almost touching. Both closed their eyes and remembered the ponies.

The two dappled grey mares were shackled to the cart for

market every Friday and she would sit high up beside Daddy on the bench, his whip in his hand. The cart would be laden with fresh eggs and home-grown vegetables to sell.

Jennie looked forward to Fridays and the freedom of the market where she could wander through the stalls selling their wares. People would smile and she could smile back, like other children.

But you weren't *other children* were you, Jennie? Nevertheless, it was a sort of freedom for a while, until dusk, when they and the cart would amble home. She would help Daddy turn the horses out into the field and watch, as, free of their shackles and harness; they would roll in the soft meadow grass.

Then, back to her tiny room in the attic, with its heavy-curtained darkness to sleep.

Or, to feign sleep, whenever the heavy footfalls were heard on the hard, wooden staircase.

No way out of the cloying darkness, Jennie! Daddy's girl - and the special gift of chocolate.

How you despise chocolate now, Jennie. How the very sight of the stuff makes the bile rise in your throat. Not unlike the burning hate you feel at the thought of the barn, with its soft hay and secret trap door to the corn-store below.

Nobody's good girl now, Jennie! The barn is bolted shut forever and silent...just like you. Not speaking, like the Trappist monks with thoughts untold; anger and pain withheld from the rest of the world.

Talk to the girl in the mirror, Jennie. She alone understands. She knows what it's like to be you - to stand in your shoes. She lives in the mirror. That is *her* world.

Her purple dress may be trendy, but it isn't able to disguise the rolls of fat around her waist and hips. The leggings are stretched to the limit precariously across bulging thighs.

Turning, Jennie looked over her shoulder at the young woman who stared back accusingly.

"Well, you ate the damn chocolate!" she spat through red, painted lips. "That's why your chins hang and your cheeks bulge. No-one forced you to eat it, Jennie. Daddy's little girl!"

Entrapment

"How dare you? Get out of my mirror, you liar!" Jennie screamed.

Mirrors *do* lie. Like those at the fairground; the ones that stretch your head and shrink your legs. The ones that pretend for a while. Like at the market, for a short time on Fridays. Pretend and smile back.

"Get out of my mirror, you lying bitch!"

The girl looked back impassively, her eyes mocking.

"You know I can't. *You* put me here Jennie. It's your fault. Everything's always been your own fault...Want some chocolate?"

Jennie shrieked and smashed her fists at the taunting image, kicking with her feet, shattering the glass into a thousand pieces. The heavy oak frame crashed to the floor with an enormous thud.

She sank to the ground, her hands still pounding the floorboards amongst the splintered mirror's fragments, oblivious to the physical pain and the blood.

Soon, people would come from the adjoining flats, alerted by the noise.

The ambulance crew would take her from the room - her prison - after tending her bleeding arms and feet. She would be wrapped in a soft blanket and carried in someone's tender arms, her four-stone, skeletal frame, enveloped with gentleness. There would be care and love and soft smiling faces.

And then the whole cycle of subtle entrapment would begin again.

Quiet Avenue
By
Carol Vardy

The red open-top MG followed the removal van slowly up Lilac Avenue. Zara and Tom glanced at each other. He pattered her arm and smiled. Already she felt at home; the surroundings made her feel relaxed. She admired the gardens full of flowers and was eager to start planting hers.

Zara said quietly,' I think we made the right decision, a new beginning. It's beautiful.'

Lilac Avenue, as the name implied, was lined with lilac trees and the sweet perfume filled the spring air. The avenue consisted of six bungalows and, apart from number five which had stood empty for three months, a widow resided in each one. Until recently the residents jokingly called themselves 'The Merry Widows.' The estate agent had mentioned to Zara that there weren't any young people living in the avenue, but she didn't mind.

Each week the widows held a coffee morning. With their families scattered around the globe their friendship with each other was important. They used to arrange days out and visits the theatre, but money had lately become scarce. They were curious, yet worried, about who was moving into number five.

'I can hear a lorry. It could be the new people.' said Joan, who lived at number four. She nervously rubbed her hands together and then clutched at her throat. Peeping around the curtain she gave a deep sigh. 'Oh thank goodness, it's not him.' Holding the curtain wider, she began a running commentary. 'It's a couple. She's just given him a kiss. They're looking this way. She's seen me. How embarrassing!' She placed her hands on her hot cheeks. 'Whatever shall I do?'

'Wave, then tell us what they look like, 'said Margery, who lived at number three. 'Are they young or old?'

'She's got long blonde hair. She's slim, about thirty, wearing tight white trousers and a yellow top,' said Joan.

Maud, the eldest of the ladies asked, 'What about him?'

'Well, he's no oil painting. He's tall, skinny, with grey hair tied in a plait down his back. He's wearing jeans and a cream shirt. Now they've linked arms. She looks years younger than him.'

'Here, let me have a look,' said Maud as she nudged Joan out of the way. 'Mm, I see what you mean; definitely younger.' She gave a loud sniff. 'Looks more like his daughter. Of course he's not my type.'

Once the removal men had gone, Zara turned and looked at the bungalows and thought how lovely and peaceful it was. Then she noticed a net curtain twitch and realized someone was waving to her. Without any hesitation Zara waved back.

Margery took a tray of drinks around to the newcomers. She smiled, introduced herself, and enquired about the man's wife. He looked puzzled.

'My wife?' he said. 'I'm a widower. This is my daughter Zara's house. I'm keeping her company until her husband's discharged from the army.'

'I reckon Margery's sweet on you. What do you think, Dad?'

'They're all nice women,' said Tom, clearing his throat and shrugging his shoulders, 'but I'm more interested in Margery's greenhouse.'He stood at the bedroom window, his binoculars trained on the object in question. 'When I asked to look inside she rapidly changed the subject. Now it's always locked. There's nothing like a mystery to get you interested. We've been here three months and she's still locking it.' He placed his arm on his daughter's shoulder. 'Sorry I've got to go away tomorrow. You'll be all right. It won't be long now before Glen will be home.'

'Don't worry, Dad. I'll be okay. I can always chat to the ladies.'

While Tom was away on business, the ladies invited Zara for tea. The table was laden with delicately cut sandwiches with a variety of fillings, and the cakes looked delicious. There was a choice of herbal teas. Zara quickly relaxed and was enjoying their company. They told her about the shows they'd seen in London, and how they always managed to get lost in the large shops. It wasn't long before they were all giggling. These ladies weren't old fuddy duddies; they knew how to have fun. Zara told them how Glen, her husband, was coming home. He'd got discharged on medical grounds. That's why she wanted a bungalow; no stairs for him to worry about.

The atmosphere changed rapidly when an unkempt, greasy-haired youth entered the room. The ladies turned pale and silent.

'Aunt Margery, I thought I'd call today. You look as though you're having a good time.' He gave her a peck on the cheek. 'Well, where is it?' Then he noticed Zara and eyed her up and down. 'New recruit?'

Margery grabbed his arm and hissed through gritted teeth. 'I'm not your aunty.' She pushed a package into his grasping hands. 'Now get out.'

Shoving him outside, she slammed and locked the door behind him.

'Come on ladies, who's for a stronger drink?' asked Maud. She tut-tutted. 'It's time we sorted him out, one way or another.'

'I know what I'd like to do with him,' said Joan as she took a good drink of the cider. 'I'm having something stronger. Anybody else for a glass of you know what?'

'You know what? I'll give it a try,' said Zara. She paused. 'Who was that? Was that money you gave him?'

The ladies went quiet, and then they turned and looked at

Margery. She nodded her head. Margery told Zara how her husband had been seriously ill. The prescribed drugs stopped working and he was in a lot of pain. They decided to grow cannabis and found that it eased his pain and added extra years to his life. After he died they decided to try the drug and found it also eased their arthritis.

'That youth.' she said with a shiver, 'used to be the window cleaner. One day I'd forgotten to close the greenhouse door. That's when he saw the contents and began to blackmail us.'

Zara smiled. 'My dad is a retired policeman. I'm sure he can help you.'

Tom nodded when Zara told him about the blackmailer. He recognised the description at once. The youth, a petty thief, was well known to the police.

'Maybe a night in the cells could be arranged,' he said. 'All the same, Margery will have to remove the cannabis plants and grow tomatoes instead.'

Neither of them knew about the plants which were flourishing in Margery's bathroom.

The ladies didn't see Zara over the following week. They knew that she wanted to fuss over Glen, now that he was finally home. However, one day she came round, needing to talk to someone who would understand. Glen wasn't sleeping very well; he kept having nightmares. Joan listened sympathetically. Then she wrapped up a piece of newly-baked cake for her friend to take home.

'See if this will help him.' Then she winked and added, 'Ask no questions.'

A few days later the young couple went to Joan's house for tea. There were the usual mouth-watering cakes and sandwiches. Glen quickly relaxed and when Tom arrived everyone was having a good laugh. He was pleased that, finally, the younger man had begun to look more at ease. In fact, Glen liked the bungalow and, having met the ladies, felt he was among friends.

'Oh, is that cake for me?' He took the plate from Margery. Then, meeting her eye, he winked. 'Doesn't it taste good?'

IS IT THE LAST TIME?
By
Graham Godfrey

Is it the first time?
Been here before
Must be the last time
This bloody war

Been here before
"Come to attention"
This bloody war
No peaceful prevention

"Come to attention"
Can we take any more?
No. Peaceful prevention?
The blood and the gore

Can we take any more?
Now the angels are dead
The blood and the gore
The cold earth their bed

Now the angels are dead
Was it worth it, this war?
The cold earth their bed
Many young dead for Thor

Was it worth it this war?
Taken in their prime
Many young dead for Thor
Is it the last time?

Love Is In The Air
By
Mary Belfield

It was Julia's first day as a fully-fledged air stewardess and she was on her inaugural flight to Italy. Taking the pilots' meals into the cockpit she found the Captain alone. He glanced up and smiled at the attractive, slim, blonde girl.

"Hello. I don't think we've met before, have we?" he asked. "I'm *sure* I would have remembered if we had!"

"No, It's my first flight," she replied, blushing at the compliment.

After introductions and some general banter about the job, the Captain's bright blue eyes twinkled as he asked, "How about me giving you a guided tour of Milan later?"

"That sounds great, thanks," said Julia.

It was the first of many 'dates'.

Six months later, during a stopover in the romantic city of Paris, Peter proposed and Julia accepted. She told him that she would love to have a formal white wedding in her local village church. Peter tried to persuade her that, to keep the costs down, they should get married on one of the Caribbean Islands they frequently visited.

"Surely, we don't have to 'penny-pinch'. We've both got secure jobs with decent salaries," she said in response.

"I know my darling, but I feel obliged to help Mum out when

I can - financially that is. She sacrificed so much to put me through flying school." He hugged his fiancée to him adding, "Don't be awkward my love. It doesn't really matter where we have the ceremony, does it? As long as we can be together."

Julia was still not fully convinced. She hadn't yet met Peter's mother who lived in the North of Scotland. She had, however, seen photographs of her with Peter's widowed sister Kirsty, and Kirsty's children, outside an extremely large house surrounded by beautiful gardens.

"What a lovely house, or perhaps mansion describes it better," she'd commented.

"Yes, but the upkeep is astronomical," he'd replied.

Julia reluctantly agreed to Peter's plans and decided to visit her parents the following weekend to tell them about their wedding arrangements. She knew her mum and dad would be very disappointed that she was not having a traditional ceremony. However, they accepted that Peter was a very caring son. Julia returned to her flat, at the end of the weekend, with a lighter heart and her parents' blessing. When she walked in she found a message on the answer phone from Peter.

"I'll be round later, sweetheart, when I get back from Scotland. Love you."

A couple of weeks later it was Peter's thirtieth birthday and Julia had planned a surprise treat for him. She'd said he should book a day's holiday and she would collect him from his flat around mid-day. Julia was up early and set off to ensure that all her plans were in place. Peter was going to have the most unusual birthday treat imaginable.

"Where're you taking me, mysterious damsel?" joked Peter as they set off. A while later he began to laugh as they drove through the gates of an old disused airfield. "What's this, 'a busman's holiday'?" he asked.

Julia simply smiled as they drew up at the door of a hangar.

"I thought that with our great love of flying this would be an appropriate treat for you. I've already had a number of sessions and found it very exhilarating."

"Not ... parachutes," Peter began to gulp but quickly changed it to a cough. "Lovely," he said leaning across and giving Julia a rather half-hearted hug.

"It's not dangerous... usually," she chuckled. "Here's my friend John, he'll take you for your initial talk and training and training while I prepare our equipment. She led Peter over to the Instructor while she entered the small door at the side of the building.

A short time later, Peter, Julia and John climbed aboard the small 'plane, Peter joking nervously that he should really be at the front of the aircraft.

"Just remember what John has taught you and you'll be fine." Attaching a tiny MP3 player to the top pocket of his flying suit she added, "There's some music and a message for my handsome birthday boy on the tape. Listen to it while you float down ...*and down ...and down*," Julia finished on a whisper.

She switched on the tape as she gave her fiancée a gentle push. In her head, she could hear the music to 'Love Is In The Air' when she stepped out. By now, the tape would have moved on to her sentimental message: "This is Goodbye...YOU RAT... from your wife Kirsty, your children Alex and Katy. And from me, your ex-loving fiancée ...Happy Birthday; Happy pulling on the rip-cord. And most of all HAPPY LANDINGS!"

As she dropped down beside the inert body of her 'ex' Julia removed the player from his Pocket. Nobody would be able to pin this on her- John had shown her exactly what to do to make it look like an 'accident'..Taking one last look at John, Julia began to cry her crocodile tears ...

Monster
By
Colyn Broom

The children watched open-mouthed, hoping that they wouldn't be seen from their hiding place as the huge monster lumbered towards them. The ground shook as it continued on its path of terror and destruction; nothing could stop it, not boulders, fences or trees. It crashed through the bushes – pausing, looking around and sniffing the air, searching almost as if it knew they were there. Steam escaped the huge sickening jaws as they opened and closed in anticipation, salivating at the thought of its next meal.

The three boys huddled together excited and terrified. The head swung around dangerously close to their little sanctuary before the beast continued its quest. With a roar, it lurched forward, head rising towards the clouds of the cool, bright, early autumn sky.

The creature had found something of interest to the left of their position, and growling, made its way towards a fallen tree. The hideous giant skull bowed low to the ground scooping up a once mighty oak with ease, tossing it to one side as though it were nothing more than a twig. With a bellowing to chill the soul, the behemoth continued its onslaught, mouth opening wide as the head tilted towards the ground. It sank massive teeth into its prey, ripping and tearing without thought or care. The boys shivered, stifling

Monster

their frightened screams so as not to give away their location. The grotesquely multi-jointed neck hoisted the head erect. Its gruesome jaws were full – too full – as pieces of the kill dribbled from the sides, spilling onto the floor. A strange smell entered the youngster's nostrils – sweet but sickly choking.

The huge monstrosity turned its bulk to stare directly at them; their breath could be seen rising in the frosty air. They had been spotted. With a deafening roar, the beast moved towards them relentless in its purpose. Gripped with fear, the boys could not move as the animal let out a terrifying cry, resembling the grating of old rusty iron door hinges. Their lungs were full of the unpleasant sulphurous stench, eardrums bursting from its shrill howl. The head bent low, as it desperately looked for a way to get at them. Should they run? *Could* they run? Was it too late anyway?

They watched wide-eyed, faces contorted with terror, as a tall man wearing a fluorescent yellow jacket and blue hat charged in front of the monster. He waved his arms, shouting to distract it from the assault. At the same, time strong hands grabbed the boys from behind.

'What the hell are you doing here?' yelled a similarly dressed figure.

The roaring of the beast had reduced to a low growl; its head lay on the ground, slain by the man in the bright jacket.

'Answer me! What are you doing here – can't you read the signs? It's a quarry not a playground.'

The three adventurers looked back at the monster. It was not moving, not breathing; they could not even hear its growl. A figure stepping out from a gaping hole in its side talked to the man in the jacket, obviously about his kill.

'One scoop full of earth from that digger would have buried you three alive,' yelled their rescuer. 'Now clear off before I send for the police!'

As the youngsters walked back down the dirt track road away from the quarry, a loud blood-curdling roar echoed from behind them. Stopping, they looked at each other.

'The beast lives!' warned the tallest, and the three boys began to run, laughing and giggling as they scurried away along the dusty trail.

Winston's Wish
By
Jean Mallender

I'm standing in my field, but it isn't quite the same,
As when *you* came.

I'll follow any bucket, if it's full of Alpha A,
I'll beat the mare to water and push her off the hay.
But when I've licked my bucket clean, and knocked it out the way,
It's not *you* gives me my mints and says to me, 'Good boy'.

I can't trot like I used to, but I swish at passing flies,
I graze and gaze, and flick my tail,
And one day, by and by...We'll meet again.
Then you can ride, for we'll be strong and free.
We'll not care where we go; there'll just be you and me.

The Decision
By
Jean Mallender

The two women sit at the kitchen table, sipping coffee and staring out of the window.

'Look at Mum, Jen, sweeping the leaves. You'd think she'd want to chat to us,' says Rose sighing. 'Did she even say hello to you? She didn't to me.'

'She smiled and pointed to the table,' Jen says. 'She's put out mugs for coffee.'

'Yes - five of them! How long is it since we were all at home? Dad's been dead two years. Anyway, where's big brother Rick? Typical - I reckon the last time he was here was the funeral.' Rose stands up, just as Rick's car pulls into the drive and he jumps out. 'Look at that, she's hugging him. We visit every few days and-'

Jen butts in: 'He lives a long way...'

'Don't make excuses...Ah! We were talking about you.'

Rose grimaces as Rick comes in and perches on a chair. 'Hi, sisters two. Why's Mum weeding the garden - we pay a gardener don't we?'

Jen sees her sister bristle and, as usual, it falls to her to forestall an argument. 'She likes it out there.'

They all stare outside at their mother - a small, bent old lady

- as she carefully rakes the gravel that surrounds a paved circle. She works on, unaware they are watching her, in a world of her own.

'Dad put that circle in, didn't he, before he died?' asks Rick.

'Yes, she'd always wanted one. Probably killed him,' added Rose.

Jen frowns. 'That's not fair. He laid it months before.'

Rose holds up her hand. 'Ok, we are here to decide, I suppose, Mum's fate.'

'She should join in.' Jen shouts out of the window: 'Mum!' But the old lady doesn't turn. 'Deaf. Not with us.'

'Yes Jen, that's the point of this exercise. Leave her, let's discuss it.'

Even Jen admits their mother is getting very frail and forgetful. Rick listens to his sisters.

When he tries to join in with, 'What about home care?' they remind him she has a morning visit already.

'Do you realise how often we call each week?' asks Rose.

'You do a grand job, girls, and if my work didn't take me abroad so often...Oh! Here she comes.' The old lady shuffles in.

'Where's your Dad?' she asks. 'I wanted to tell him...' The rest is lost as she carries on into the sitting room.

They follow to find her in her armchair, groping for her spectacles. She focuses on them for the first time, her eyes flashing from one to the other. 'I don't want to leave my home.'

'Oh, so you *do* remember what we are going to talk about?' Rose nods at Jen for backup.

'Mum - we worry about you.'

The old woman turns to Rick. 'Is this why you've come?'

Rick bends over her. 'We think it's getting hard for you to cope.'

'Where's your Dad? I've not seen him all day.'

Rick turns to his sisters shaking his head.

'Anyway, I'm staying here,' she says. 'This.. is.. where.. we.. live.' Her fists beat out the rhythm of the words on the chair arms. Then her expression softens as she looks round. 'Now, off to bed the three of you. I'll be in the garden with your Dad.'

She heaves herself up and goes out once more, ignoring their protests.

'Have you noticed she keeps a rake and sweeping brush beside the back door?' asks Rose.

Jen nods. 'She cleans the circle, as she calls it, daily - even in the rain. Dad loved the garden and she loved him.'

They decide to leave things as they are for a bit longer, with more help from the carer. The girls will take it in turns to call daily and Rick promises, as he goes, to visit more often.

'At least she never wanders off,' Jen says. 'The garden keeps her here.'

They persuade her to come in for her tea before they leave.

The old lady goes out again that night. She doesn't mind the rain, or the dark. She sits on the seat, next to the circle, and dreams. It is she who decides what will happen, in the end.

The Park
By
Leonie Martin

The boy drains another can before hurling it through the railings and into the black void beyond. Heaving his limbs up and over, he forgets about the bushes on the other side.

'*Shit!*' His voice echoes around the deserted park. Slumped in the hazy lamp-light, he can make out a razor-sharp thorn embedded in his arm. As a warm trickle of blood begins to ooze down his wrist, he is seized by a childhood memory:

He is eight-years-old. 'King of the Swings' at the park. One minute the elusive clouds are just inches away from his outstretched legs; the next, he is sprawled on the tarmac nursing a deep gash to his shin. Blood surfaces quickly; a crimson stain soaks his torn jeans.

'Try and keep still, David,' says a calm voice at his side. He feels his grandfather's hand; warm upon his shoulder. An enormous white handkerchief appears from one of the countless pockets in Gramps' faded overalls. 'Let's tie this around your leg – it'll stop the blood.'

Slumped in the night-time shadows, he can still recall Gramps' reassuring blue eyes. And despite the throbbing in his arm, the memory brings a weak smile to his pallid face. The old man had a cure for everything: herbal ointments to sooth insect bites; steaming potions to chase away colds; liquorice to calm stomach aches. Then, his smile vanishes. Yes: a cure for everything except his only daughter's drink problem. David's jaw tightens as his mother's screaming, red face and toxic breath flash before him. But a cooling breeze strokes his face and the shushing sound of leaves high above his head sooth his mind. He is safe in the park. She can't hurt him here.

He breathes in deeply, drawing strength from the earthy smell of night air. It had been impossible to sleep in his suffocating bedsit; to escape the scenes from yesterday's grim procession: the long, black cars; that greedy hole swallowing his grandfather. Here, in familiar surroundings, he feels close to the memory of the one person who'd accepted and loved him without question. The park is David's thinking space. Here, he knows what to expect; whatever the season. And tonight, he'll be with Gramps once again.

A few feet away a path slopes towards the play area. As he tries to stand, the world tilts in front of him, sending him reeling back into the bushes. A huddle of panic-stricken ducks scatters towards the boating-lake. Grabbing a thick branch for support, he pulls himself back up, catching his breath in painful gulps. The sound of cars whizzing past on the dual carriageway make his head turn: people with homes to go to. Snatches of music and laughter float from clubs and pubs across town: people celebrating. Sinking to the ground, he takes the last can from his jacket pocket, ripping at the ring-pull. Hot tears mingle with blood and froth as he lifts it to his chapped lips and lets the memories flow.

'Penny for them, David?' Gramps would often ask as they watched the cricket. They always sat on the same bench – near that old statue of a young girl with a rose. At the time, he hadn't really understood what his grandfather meant by those words. He does now. But nobody offers him pennies any more. A choking sound tears from his throat at the memory of the dark-wood coffin disappearing behind that red, velvet curtain. Kicking a stone against a nearby tree, he takes another swig and checks his pocket. Yes; it's still there; his one-way ticket from this world.

A distant, wailing siren goads him, causing his softly-stubbled face to mask over in the darkness. He hears a rustling noise in the early-autumn carpet and looks up. It becomes louder; more of a crunch than a rustle. Then it stops. He tenses, adrenalin lessening the effects of the lager. There it is again. Grabbing a stone, he springs up and takes aim. A crunch of foot on dry twig; a dark shape on the ground, edging nearer...he feels the sweat, cold on his brow. And then relief, as a young fox pads into the moon-lit clearing and regards him with a flash of amber, before melting back into the darkness with a flick of its white-tipped tail.

In a rush of clarity, he unclenches his fist and lets the stone fall to the ground. He begins to laugh; a hollow laugh that shakes his body, making tears course down his face. Realisation washes over him. Never in his life has he felt so free. The sensation makes him light-headed; giddy with anticipation. When the laughter finally subsides, he sinks down on the carpet of leaves and soaks up the silence.

Over to his left, the park's model railway runs parallel to a nearby path before branching off between the trees, its narrow tracks coming to an abrupt end at a pair of strong, wooden gates. He used to ride the little train with his grandfather; the two of them making up names for the ducks and sipping *Coca Cola* from a can. All that is gone now: ruined. Just like that picture he spent ages drawing on those long, lonely weekends before Gramps had stepped into his life.

David's picture had begun as way of killing time when his step-brother and step-sister were out. Ashley and Jade both had Dads who turned up at weekends with sweets; presents; hugs. He'd never known his father, who his mother usually referred to as, *'that Bastard'*.

Watching from his bedroom window David would imagine how it felt to be Ashley, climbing into the seat of his dad's truck; or giggling Jade on her way to the park in her father's rusty, blue Astra. On those long, lonely weekends, he did his best to be invisible: either out in the junk-filled garden or up in his bedroom, while his mother kept the curtains drawn and the TV on; empty bottles piling up at the end of the sofa like dirty, glass skittles.

Not having a father was one thing. What made it worse was the fact that he looked nothing like the rest of his dark-haired family.

'Bet your Dad was a 'ginner'!' the kids at school would goad him; pointing at his red hair and pale, freckled skin.

They would snigger when he struggled to read in class. Letters just wouldn't come together in the right order for him, dancing about on the page until a red mist filled his head, blocking everything out. When his teachers tried to talk to his mother about it, she had a go at him.

'Typical! Thick as pig-shit you are.'

One weekend, while Ashley and Jade were away, he opened his curtains to find that the view from his window changed. The old lady next door had recently died and there was now a mucky yellow skip on the drive, overflowing with junk. The next day, he got up early and rummaged around in it, finding amongst other things a half-used roll of plain wall-paper. He smuggled it upstairs and crawled underneath his bed to reach his secret box. This was where he kept things he didn't want his mother to see: like the birthday card from his grandfather. The card had a picture of a park with a cricket pitch, a boating lake, and a boy on roller-skates wearing a shirt with a red number seven. She'd destroyed all the other cards before he'd even seen them and hadn't spoken to her father for years.

'Doesn't he get the message?' she'd roar at the letterbox.

On his seventh birthday she'd been in bed with a hangover when the post arrived. There'd been a parcel from his grandfather. He managed to sneak it upstairs, ripping open the brown paper as quietly as his trembling hands would allow. As well as the card, he found a colouring box, felt tips, wax crayons and pencils of every shade. He'd been saving it for a something special, and finding the wallpaper had given him an idea. Unfurling the roll and placing a slipper at either end to keep it flat, he chose from the rainbow of colours in the box and began to draw.

Gradually, over the weeks, David created his own park. It had a massive play-area with the tallest, steepest, shiniest slide;

bright coloured swings that went so high you could touch the clouds with your feet. His favourite part was the boating lake, with a whole fleet of painted wooden boats on a smooth turquoise surface. There was lime-green grass for football and cricket. In the middle was a bandstand where one day brass bands would play happy music for the crowds. Not yet though; his park wasn't ready for people. Around the grass were tall, thin trees, and multi-coloured flower-bushes with petals that looked like delicious, sticky sweets.

Hours would fly past as he lost himself in his imaginary park; until his mother broke the spell.

'David!' she'd yell. 'Stop hiding. Take the bloody dogs out – you lazy little sod.'

On his eighth birthday, the doorbell rang early. As usual, he was the only one up and raced downstairs in his *Batman* pyjamas, almost tripping over a pile of empty bottles in the cluttered porch as he tugged open the door.

'Where are we going today then, young David?' boomed a voice. The doorway was filled by the figure of a tall, silver-haired man. Something about him looked familiar – as if from a long-forgotten photograph. 'It's your birthday,' said the man, his blue eye's twinkling, 'today *you* get to decide.'

'David?' he heard his Mum yell. 'Who is it?'

'It's...It's...'

'Granddad,' said the big man, grinning.

David heard footsteps thundering down the stairs and stood in wide-eyed silence.

'What the –' gasped his mother, clutching at her grubby, towelling dressing-gown.

'Surprise!' said the man. 'Close your mouth and put the kettle on, Stacey; you and I need to talk.'

David trembled. Nobody dared talk to his mother like that. He glanced around, automatically dipping his head for protection, but felt a large, warm hand settle on his shoulder like a cloak.

'I've come to take the lad out for his birthday', said the man, 'and to tell you I've moved back to town. You'll not stop me seeing him. Any trouble and social services will find out what really goes on here.' His eyes took in the empty bottles littering the floor.

That day was to be the first of many outings with his grandfather. For the first time in David's life he felt connected. Someone cared about what he liked; disliked; what made him tick. As they wandered through the big park in town, Gramps would do his best to keep up with the boy's endless questions:

'Why are leaves green?'
'What makes conkers round and shiny?'
'Why do flowers smell? '

They'd feed the ducks and go to the play-park, sharing jokes and crunching on Gramps' never ending supply of butter-mints.

'One day...' squealed David as Gramps pushed his swing ever higher, '...I'll reeeeach the clouds!'

Sadly, life at school was a different matter: things had sunk to an all time low and he'd been put on report for fighting. He didn't know how to tell Gramps – he'd recently noticed a limp in the old man's step as they walked, and although he never complained, David could see pain in his blue eyes.

Once Ashley and Jade became teenagers they were too busy for outings with their Dads. But David and Gramps still went to the park. A little café opened and if the weather was bad they'd chat over mugs of sweet tea and munch chips and cheese with plenty of ketchup. When it was fine, they'd wander round enjoying the best of each season: ducklings bobbing in the lake; the reassuring sound of bat on ball; leaves crunching underfoot; the sharp, clear air of a crisp winter's day.

One summer, as they sat on the bench throwing breadcrumbs to the birds, David owned up to his grandfather about the trouble he'd been in at school.

The creases around the old man's eyes seemed to deepen.

'Don't get yourself labelled, David. You're a good lad.' He ran a hand through his silver hair. 'When you're sixteen, I'll sort you out an apprenticeship – I've a mate who'll take you on: he's got a gardening business. A lad like you needs to work outdoors: plenty of freedom.'

It was his grandfather who'd pleaded with the police when he was caught stealing from the corner shop. David had hung his head: he'd been stealing vodka for his mother, but couldn't bring himself to tell the truth or Ashley and Jade would hate him too.

'He's a good kid really,' Gramps had told the officers. 'It's his parents – Dad's never been on the scene. And his mother…all those kids… different dads; the house is a tip; they never know where the next meal's coming from. The government gives her money, but she spends most of it on booze and fags. Just wish I'd lived nearer before now,' he said with a sigh. 'I knew things weren't good at home, but I'd no idea…'

The police were fair, but they had procedures to follow; targets to meet. David was just one of many. An officer with pale-blue lapels on his white shirt took David's fingerprints and scraped plastic swabs inside his cheeks. His DNA was now stamped for life: Do Not Allow. Neither his grandfather, nor the tall man in the black suit standing silently in the corner of the interview room could wind the tape back and erase the stain on his character. Returning from the police station that night, something made him search for the park picture beneath his bed. He hadn't looked at it for ages. Taking it in his hands, he tore at it in a wild frenzy, shredding it into tiny pieces that fluttered fell around his sobbing form.

Alone in the park, David is surer than ever of his course of action. Now his grandfather's big heart has stopped beating he no longer wants to be part of this world. He staggers out from the bushes clutching his arm and heads for the swings. Weaving past a bench where the statue used to stand he hears a noise and pauses. A strong smell of roses suddenly fills the air.

'*Penny for them?*' calls a voice.

It sounds like a child's voice, high-pitched and soft. He squeezes his arm. Maybe the wound is deeper than he thought? Taking a deep breath he continues walking.

'Penny for them?' repeats the voice. It's coming from the direction of the old conservatory.

He turns.

'Please don't leave,' says the voice. 'Don't leave me.'

It's an odd, old-fashioned accent. He hesitates.

'I've picked you,' the voice continues. 'There's something…something I need you to do.'

'Who – who is this?' he calls, the hairs on his arms bristling.

'I used to see you in the park; watching cricket with a silver-haired gentleman.'

David's heart thumps so loudly it seems to echo in the darkness.

'Where are you?'

'Over here.'

The moon dips behind a bank of clouds.

'Where's here?'

'Can you see the potting shed – by the conservatory?'

He feels his feet move.

The conservatory is ancient: more gaps than glass between its splintered frames. Next to it is an old brick building where the park-keepers store broken equipment and tools.

'Do you have a lamp?' asks the voice.

'*Lamp*?'

'You'll struggle to see me without one.'

He reaches in his jacket pocket for his lighter. And feels the small, foil package: his one-way ticket.

'I don't think–'

'Please!' The voice sounds choked with emotion.

He removes the lighter.

'Nearer,' urges the voice, 'behind the shed.'

It suddenly occurs to him that this might be a trick – the sort of sick joke they used to play on him at school. He hesitates again.

'I remember the time you fell from the swing,' cries the voice into the clear night air. 'You wounded your leg - and the old gentleman looked after you.'

David begins to tremble. Hot tears build behind his eyes.

'I too can help you. But first, you need to find me. Use your lamp.'

He takes a deep breath and moves towards the brick building, almost tripping on a discarded flower-pot. Behind it is a stone wall. There's a gap between the two structures – just a bit wider than his shoulders. He squeezes in and holds up his lighter, flicking it with his thumb. In the light of the tiny flame it's hard to see much.

'I'm here – in the corner.'

He lifts the lighter and leans forward. What he sees in the flicker of the flame takes him straight back to those summer days with his granddad. The statue of the Rose Girl, lying on its side, partially covered with weeds and long grass.

'It's me,' says the statue. 'Alice.'

David bites his tongue hard to check if he's dreaming. The taste of blood in his mouth tells him he isn't.

'I *must* get out of here,' pleads the statue. 'Will you help me?'

The lighter is beginning to burn him. He takes his thumb off the lever and the flame splutters and dies.

'Shit!' He sticks the singed thumb in his mouth.

The girl begins to cry; small, piercing sobs.

'Wait a minute,' he says, 'let me think. And please…stop crying?'

Leaning on an old roller, he waits for the sobs to reduce to sniffles. Swapping hands, he flicks the lighter again.

'Right…Alice,' he hears himself say. 'What do you want me to do? And how can *you* possibly help *me*?'

'I'm not meant to be here,' says the statue.

'What do you mean?'

'I should be over there – in front of the silver birch tree. That's where my father meant for me to stand.'

'Your father…?'

'Yes. There's a story. When I was three-years-old I picked a rose from our garden – Father caught me hiding it behind my back. It made him smile. I had to stand still while he sketched me. Then he took a stone gate post from our farm and carved my statue.'

'Clever man,' David murmurs, wondering where this is leading.

'Oh, he was; and kind. He knew all about plants and animals.

The Park

He loved cricket too – that's why he bequeathed me to the park; on condition that I must always stand in front of the silver birch tree, overlooking the cricket pitch.'

'So...how did you end up here?'

'Last year, the old park-keeper died; he'd been here fifty years and always looked after me. The new man – he had other ideas. He promised to restore the conservatory so they gave him lots of money. I knew he was a rogue – I saw how cruelly he treated the ducks. I never spoke to him, but he could tell I was watching – and one night he came and moved me. I've been here ever since. Shortly after, he ran off with all the money.'

'But you're a statue,' he says. 'Statues don't speak...'

'My father had a unique gift – he was able to communicate with the natural world. When he carved me, he imparted his spirit. It enabled me to fulfil his wishes. My spirit is now the spirit of the park.'

David's arm throbs painfully. This is too much.

'Why me?'

'I've been watching you for a long time. And the silver-haired gentleman – I could tell he was a kind man: the right person to replace the park-keeper. But he was too old. And then I saw that you had the same qualities; endurance; loyalty; imagination. But you were too young. All this time I've been waiting; willing you to return to take over the job and put things right.'

'*Me*? I'm trouble. That's all people ever tell me.'

'You've been speaking to the wrong people. The man – your grandfather; he left you his spirit and his passion for nature.' Her voice falters a moment before continuing. 'Believe in yourself, David. Do as I tell you.'

He shivers.

'I can't move you on my own – you're too heavy.'

'Go home now; bathe your wound and rest. Be at the conservatory for midday tomorrow. Wear your finest clothes.'

'*Finest clothes?*' he says, 'I've only got jeans?'

'I don't know what you speak of – but if they're your finest, they'll do. Go now - and trust me. All will be well.'

As he climbs back over the fence, he can hear the first strains of the morning chorus from the treetops around the lake.

David wakes the next day with the mother of all headaches. Throwing a couple of pain-killers down, he crawls back under his duvet with a groan. The more last night's drama attempts to filter through his consciousness, the harder he fights to stop it. *Talking bloody statues?* People were right – he was mad; a loser.

Eventually, hunger gets the better of him. Swinging his legs round he sits up, rubbing his eyes. First, he notices his clothes strewn on the worn carpet; then the unopened envelope he left on the bedside table before escaping to the park last night. On the front he'd scribbled his mother's name and address. He blinks. What had really happened last night? And why did he no longer feel that hollow ache in his chest? He picks up his mobile: 11.15 a.m. Maybe he should turn up at the conservatory – not that he believed anything would happen of course – but he could check if the statue was still behind the potting shed.

At 11.45 he finds himself treading the familiar path through the park. It's a Monday; pensioners throw bread to the ducks and parents push toddlers on swings. Everything looks greener, fresher to him somehow; the reds and pinks of the rose bushes more vibrant. As he nears the conservatory he notices a tall man in a dark suit standing by the door, holding a briefcase. He looks vaguely familiar. The man looks up and catches his eye.

'David,' he says, holding out his hand, 'pleased to meet you. Let's go in and sit down.'

He follows the man inside.

They occupy an ancient, iron bench to one side of the splintered double doors and the man opens his briefcase.

'Thank you for filling in the paperwork, David. It's all in order. Your references are excellent; you have all the right connections.' He meets David's barely-concealed astonishment with a steady, brown gaze. 'When can you start? As you know, the position is vacant; jobs are stacking up. There's a lot to be done before winter arrives.'

The Park

'I can't,' he replies, his whole body trembling. 'The police...my criminal record...'

He feels a warm hand on his arm. 'Trust me. It's all been sorted out; report to the Park Development Officer in the main building tomorrow morning at nine. No need to mention our meeting today; they're expecting you.'

David opens his mouth to speak but nothing comes out. He feels something brush across his arm, like a spider's web. He glances down to find that the angry wound from the previous night is completely healed. For a few seconds he just stares, transfixed. When he looks up again the man has vanished.

The following day he starts his new job. As weeks and months turned into years, he becomes a well-known and popular figure in the park. Throughout every season he works hard: pruning, digging, planting, and all the other tasks required to preserve this picture of peace: a place where residents of the town can feel relaxed, safe and happy. People stroll past and comment on the newly restored statue of the Rose Girl. David often sits on the nearby bench to eat his sandwiches and throw crumbs. If passers-by hear him talking, they assume he's chatting to the birds.

Unfinished History

By
Rosie Gilligan

Paul screwed up his nose. 'What *is* that smell?'

Anna pointed to the clusters of green and white flowers above their heads. 'It's the blossom on the trees. Linden blossom.' The helpful reply hid her irritation with the question – but she would concede if pressed that the sharp, sweet aroma *was* overpowering.

It was nearly midday and very hot. The sticky, sap-filled green leaves formed a welcome canopy as they walked towards the end of the boulevard. There they hesitated, reluctant to step out into the searing heat of the city.

'Do you have the guidebook?' Paul asked.

Anna rummaged in her bag. 'Damn! I must have left it in the car.'

He frowned. '*That's* useful.'

It was too far to go back now and fetch it. 'I *can* remember some bits,' she said, putting on her hat and sunglasses. She wasn't confident of this, and was cross about forgetting it.

Paul sighed. 'Let's get lunch.'

They found a restaurant in the main square and sat under a huge umbrella, sipping cold drinks and waiting for their food to arrive. They watched the quiet, empty space. Just a few tourists were out, dodging the midday heat and crossing to the shade on the other side.

'So, where are we?' Paul said, after a lengthy silence. He gave Anna a searching look.

'Right,' she said, hoping she could recall what she'd read during this morning's journey, 'this is Brezovica, population about 50,000, capital of Crovania. The country gained independence from … from what remained of the Yugoslav Federation in 2006. The last king – Nikolai II – lived here. I think that's his Palace over there,' she said, pointing straight ahead.

Paul looked at the two-storied building whose frontage occupied one side of the square. It was painted a deep red and boasted an imposing porch, with numerous tall windows either side. Their white stone mouldings shone brilliantly in the sun.

'When was it built?'

'Er … about 1850. It's in the Empire style, influenced by Napoleon III – very popular across Europe at the time.' She felt she was doing quite well without the guidebook.

'So what happened to Nikolai II, then?'

This question was trickier. 'Murdered by … I forget who,' she said. Something about this unlucky monarch was lodged at the back of her mind, and she wished she could consult the guidebook. 'It's very peaceful here now, but in the past there were so many factions … so many ethnic groups.'

She was rescued by the arrival of lunch. Paul had pasta and Anna steak and French fries. She picked at her food. The meat was tender and sweet, but it had been barely seared on the outside. A thin, watery blood seeped across the plate and into the fries.

'Where do you want to go this afternoon?' Paul asked, as they finished lunch.

She'd been anticipating the question. It meant he was bored and didn't give a damn about what they did. And it put the responsibility on her to make all the decisions – and take the blame if it went wrong. 'I don't know,' she said. 'It's too hot to do much.' The reality was she wanted to lie on a bed, in a cool room, and sleep. But there was little prospect of that for the next few hours.

She looked across the square to Nikolai's Palace. 'Let's wander over there.'

'Museu Narodni Historica Crovanski,' Paul read from the sign at the front of the building. 'I wonder if that means "The National Historical Museum of Crovania". Do you fancy?'

Anna shrugged. 'If you like.'

Paul held open one of the heavily-moulded wooden doors under the porch, and they entered. Inside, the temperature immediately dropped ten degrees. They walked across a stained marble floor, towards a shabby wooden desk. On the other side sat a lady with bleached blonde hair, wearing a bright red overall. She sold them tickets, and beckoned them to follow her through further wooden doors to their left.

After the blinding light of the square outside, Anna could at first see very little. Gradually she realised they were in a huge, rectangular room running along the front of the palace. Straight ahead, and to her left, thin shafts of light sliced through the edges of curtains drawn across three tall windows. Then she saw spotlights shining weakly downwards from the ceiling onto a row of glass display cases in the centre of the room.

'Prehistorici,' the lady said, smiling proudly. She pointed at a paper notice stuck to the glass on the first case. 'Angliski.'

'Ah yes!' they said, nodding together. The displays were evidently arranged in chronological order. *And* there were explanations in English. The lady smiled. Her work done, she retreated to the foyer.

They peered into the first case. There was a scruffy label on the glass, which was coming unstuck at one end. It was printed on cheap photocopying paper, and it informed them its contents were finds from "the Lukovici cave, where the Beaker Persons lived". Inside the case were shards of pottery, pieces of bone, and drawings of huts on stilts.

'I'm glad they didn't bother to go to too much trouble with the translations,' Anna said, smiling ruefully. 'It's *so* tiring having to deal with all this foreign history.'

Paul grimaced and peered into the case, before moving swiftly on.

Now her eyes had become accustomed to the low light level, Anna turned full circle, surveying her surroundings. They were in what she thought must once have been a stateroom, although few traces were left of its original splendour. The walls were panelled in wood; the chandeliers that might originally have hung there were missing from the two ornate plaster roses in the ceiling. She looked down and saw a threadbare and dusty carpet covering most of the floor. Underneath were parquet tiles in a herringbone pattern.

Anna followed Paul to the second case. It contained stone and shell beads "made into Jewels, for trade, by the Illyrian speaker-tribes, 8th century BC". There were maps showing where the finds were discovered, and it was clear that the region was rich in prehistory. Anna thought that the people who lived in this remote corner of the Balkans must have been as advanced as those at home. She turned to Paul to speak to him, but saw she was alone; he had already moved through the open doors at the end, and into the next room.

A surge of irritation coursed through her; this was what he always did. He never studied things properly, preferring to race ahead. He wouldn't be far away – just far enough to prevent her sharing her thoughts and discoveries with him. She would either have to find him and pull him back, or race to catch him up and miss whole chunks of the museum.

Sighing, she moved on to the third case. Inside were small finds from excavations, such as arrow heads, "evidence of gory fightings against Ostrogoths, Turki and Franks". But she barely glanced at them – or at any of the other objects in the room. Her annoyance with Paul had disrupted her concentration.

Room Two was even larger. As she entered, Paul was already at the other end. He glanced back, before disappearing into the next room. She ignored him and moved towards the first case. "Clay people of the Roman times, 2nd Century," the label declared. The terracotta figures inside were identical to those they had seen in Rome and Florence. She would have liked to know more about these delightfully playful statues, but the information – in Crovanian – was impossible to understand. The second case contained oil lamps and fragments of glass bowls. She looked in vain for an English explanation but there was none – not on this case, nor on any of the others in the room. Whoever began this translation project had quickly lost interest. She shrugged and briefly considered leaving, but by now Paul would be even further ahead. It was easier just to carry on. And peering out of the window through a gap in the curtain, seeing the bright, empty street, she was reminded about how hot it would still be outside.

Anna moved into Room Three and had to turn right. She was progressing along the side of the building. Meandering past cases full of fragments of pottery and metal tools, she only briefly scanned the contents. It was almost a pleasure to be relieved of the effort of having to take it all in. Then her eyes began to glaze over and, as she made for Room Four, she was suddenly hit by a wave of fatigue that made her buckle at the knees.

There was nowhere to sit – no benches or chairs. Anna sank to the floor by the wall. At some stage in every holiday – and especially those involving complicated travel arrangements to inaccessible places – a deep weariness usually set in. She loved the *idea* of foreign travel, but the reality was that strange sights, sounds and tastes – and uncomfortable hotel beds – exhausted her within a few days.

The building was so quiet she could hear its faint creaks and ticks. Nothing moved, apart from dust motes caught in slivers of sunlight. There appeared to be no other visitors, and the cases were as lifeless as sarcophagi. She felt like a slave, incarcerated in a tomb with deceased royalty – waiting for rescue, but knowing it would never come. Anna closed her eyes and considered all the events in her life that had led her to this place, on this day.

A sound like machine gun fire made her jump. She opened her eyes. It was so distant she could have been mistaken, but it made her feel anxious. She stood up, dusting off her shorts. Her resentment at having been abandoned by Paul rose again. They had been married for 30 years and his habit of racing ahead was intensifying; she suspected he no longer cared about her. She suddenly felt the need to confront him when she caught up, but knew he would sulk. And afterwards there was no chance she could give him a wide berth; holidays always threw them together into the confined space of a hotel bedroom.

She turned another corner and assumed she was now at the back of the building, which was in the shade. Room Four was long, narrow and dark. It was lined with tall cases. They formed an imposing corridor down which she had to progress to reach the other end of the room. Inside were bunches of wooden staves, topped with metal spikes, menacing looking swords, and wooden shields and crests. It was a collection of medieval relics: evidence of a country in turmoil; of clans and tribes and bitter fighting. There were maps explaining – but only to Crovanian speakers – movement of armies and state boundaries across the region. She looked ahead towards the end of the room. Perhaps it was her imagination, but it appeared to narrow disconcertingly. Anna quickened her pace, her tired legs struggling to make progress along the shabby carpet.

Room Five was huge, and she guessed it was once a ballroom. The floor was bare and it creaked slightly as she crossed it. She had hoped to find Paul, but he was still out of sight.

She wasn't alone. The cases were positioned evenly throughout the room and contained crudely made manikins with painted-on faces. They gaped provocatively at her. The males sported homespun shirts, leather trousers, embroidered waistcoats, and elaborate felt hats with feathers. The females – less flamboyant – wore plain skirts and simple blouses under thick capes and wraps. There was something uneasy about their bearing – as if they were alive, and had been required to freeze into awkward postures because she was passing through. One male had his arms raised, as if making a futile attempt to escape from his confines; elsewhere, a female was leaning drunkenly against the glass inside her case.

'You don't scare me one little bit – none of you,' Anna muttered under her breath. She swallowed hard, trying not to show her agitation, but her heart raced with anxiety; this wasn't a room to visit alone. The mocking gaze of the room's inhabitants reminded her of the House of Horrors at the fair.

The sound of machine guns again punctured the air. This time it was louder. Avoiding the eyes staring insolently at her from the last few cases, she quickly entered Room Six. It was at right angles to the last, and she thought she must now be at the other side of the building.

It was brighter here. Welcome shafts of sunlight seeped in and onto a multitude of cases filled with maps, documents and photographs – enough clues for her to guess the room's focus was the 19th century. There were lengthy scripts outlining – but not for her – the complexities of Balkan political and social history. The exhibits and the explanatory notes were faded, the colours drained by strong sunlight and the passage of time. Anna wondered how long it had been since anything in the museum had been changed or refreshed. With its lifeless tableaux imprisoned in dusty glass cases, the museum itself was a museum-piece. It was a discovery that left her feeling cheated somehow.

She was about to enter the next room when something near the door caught her eye. A military tunic – be-ribboned, be-medalled, and heavy with gold braid – stood almost alone in a case. It had once been white, but was now yellowed with age. A brown stain, and a hole the size of a tomato in the upper left quarter, suggested the wearer had been mortally wounded. Intrigued, Anna approached and studied the photographs next to it. Dark eyes stared back at her from a youthful, angular face; this handsome young man could only be King Nikolai II.

Now she remembered what she had read in the guidebook: caught between the Austro-Hungarian Empire to the north and the Turkish Empire to the south, Crovania had long been an unstable country. Nikolai II's father had encouraged the first seeds of democracy 20 years earlier. But the supporters of the People's Party had been impatient. On the day in 1907 when Nikolai II ascended the throne, they seized their chance to change their destiny. The guidebook had described in graphic detail how a small group of rebels had entered the Palace through an upper window during the King's coronation celebrations. The assembled congregation had watched in horror as Nikolai – just an hour into his reign – was shot in the heart whilst raising a toast to his countrymen; he was 26 years old.

The *rat-tat-tat* of machine gun fire sounded again, much closer. Alarmed, Anna decided it was time to find Paul and leave. She quickly opened the door to Room Seven and was plunged into a dark, enclosed space. Loud explosions burst from above and lights flashed in her eyes. There was nowhere to go but through a hot, narrow tunnel straight ahead. She entered reluctantly, groping her way along the rough walls as it turned first one way, then the other. She thought it would go on forever. Then she stumbled and fell. Panic-stricken, and with tears blurring her vision, she cried out, scrambled up, and dashed towards the light ahead. She pushed against a swing door and burst, bathed in sweat, into Room Eight.

Wiping her face with the back of her hand, Anna tried to take in the surroundings. It was a large, dark room with plate glass windows down opposite sides. Inside them were illuminated dioramas of uniformed manikins fighting bravely in battle – or hunkering down in dugouts. In the centre of the room was a long wooden bench. And lying along it, on his back, was Paul. He was fast asleep and snoring.

Anna screamed and threw her bag at him. It missed and hit the carpet with a dull thud, and a puff of dust.

Paul sat up, blinking, struggling to focus. 'What the …?'

'You make me *sick*!' she cried. 'How *dare* you rush off? You don't give a *damn* about me!'

He rose and slowly approached her. Cautiously he stretched out his arms and cocked his head on one side. 'Don't be silly, Anna. I was just tired. I had no idea–'

'You *never* do. I might as well not be here, all the notice you ever take of me.' Hot tears ran down her face which she made no attempt to stem. Paul tried to embrace her, but his touch was the last thing she wanted. She flicked her arms outwards. 'Get away from me. I don't want to see you *ever* again. I want a divorce.'

He stood in front of her. She couldn't see him properly through her tears, but she knew his eyes were scanning her face, searching to understand.

'Anna, I'm *so* sorry. You must have been *very* frightened. Please forgive my thoughtlessness,' he said, in hushed tones.

'*Don't* patronise me,' she said, glaring, her anger hardly abated.

There was another burst of machine gun fire. Anna looked up. On the upper walls and ceiling, an army was marching through the snow.

Paul's eyes followed hers. 'It's a sound and light show – about the First and Second World Wars,' he explained. His voice was almost calm; he was trying to sound normal. 'Here, let's sit down and watch. It lasts about ten minutes.' He took hold of her rigid arm and slowly coaxed her towards the bench.

They sat together, silent and unmoving. Anna's brain felt numb. She barely took in the complex array of sounds and images that played over the peeling plasterwork on the curved ceiling. Fighting and marching men came from all directions. Convoys of tanks ploughed by. Half-familiar political figures made impassioned speeches to ecstatic crowds, while peasants wailed as they watched their homes burning. She understood none of it, yet she had seen it a hundred times before, on news channels and in documentaries.

As the room fell quiet again, she turned to Paul. 'How can a country the size of Wales have *this* much history?' she asked. For some reason she couldn't explain, even that made her angry. She rose and walked to the door to Room Nine.

Paul followed. It was another large room. Huge, faded flags were pinned to the wall. Alongside, framed photographs celebrated the rise of Tito and four decades of Communism. There were cases full of maps, medals and hundreds of incomprehensible documents.

Something caught Paul's attention and he turned to her. 'Anna, come and look at this … *please.*'

Anna had gone to the other side of the room, to be as far away from him as possible. He beckoned her over and she approached slowly. In the case were photographs of factories and industrial production. He pointed to one, showing a line of cars.

'Look; the Yugo,' he said, 'once described as the worst car in the world. Do you remember my father had one?'

The sound of machine guns started again. Anna grimaced at the photograph, unwilling to rise to Paul's lame attempt at reconciliation. 'Let's go. Surely we *must* be near the end.' She pushed open the door to Room Ten and stepped inside.

This one was large and empty. The plasterwork on the ceiling was depositing off-white flakes on another dusty carpet. Anna walked to the middle of the room and twirled. She resisted the urge to laugh out loud.

'What is it?' asked Paul. He stood hesitantly in the doorway, one hand on the frame.

'It's all a con,' she said, now rotating slowly, one arm outstretched. 'What about the Balkan Wars? Did Mostar and Srebrenica never happen? Were Milosevich and Karadadjic never indicted for the massacres and the bombings? This is unfinished history. I don't think anyone has been in here – except us – in the past 20 years.'

'Perhaps they're just renovating this room,' said Paul, walking slowly towards her.

She gave him a withering look. 'Let's go. I need to get back to reality.'

Without waiting for his response, she pushed open the door and found herself out in the coolness of the empty marble foyer. The exit was straight ahead. She strode across towards it.

'Here, let me.' Paul raced in front of her and opened the heavy, moulded doors.

Outside, the sun was still high in the sky. They stood in the shade of the elaborate and imposing porch, squinting into the blinding light. Anna searched for her hat and sunglasses. She found them and, in the few seconds it took to put them on, Paul set off across the empty square. Speechless, she stood and watched as the distance between them grew. Yet again he'd pressed on without her.

The explosions came from nowhere. Their deafening *crack, crack, crack* stunned her, and she froze. She watched Paul slowly crumple forwards, then fall to one side. Anna's legs turned to jelly;

the journey she took to be with him seemed to last forever.

He lay unmoving on the hot tarmac. There was something wrong with his left shoulder, and his arm was twisted behind his back at an impossible angle. A dark, terrifying stain was spreading outwards from the upper left quadrant of his shirt, and down onto the ground. Anna kneeled beside him and cupped her hands over it. She knew it was probably a futile gesture, but she thought it might be worth trying to scoop the blood back into his body.

She opened her mouth, but was unable to utter a word. Looking up and towards the restaurant where they had eaten lunch, she realised that the large umbrella, and the tables and chairs, were gone. Then she saw men in uniform – too many to count – positioned behind a line of grey jeeps and tanks at the edge of the square ...

Inevitability
By
Phil Foster

The night-revellers swayed, intoxicated by the onslaught of an invisible yet awesome enemy. Their ranks were united as they heaved their snow-covered, leaden upper limbs against the elemental powers. A vestige of pride and discipline urged each member to give one last "Big Push", "a snappy salute" only to be cowed once more by superior forces.

Surrender was inevitable: the battle was lost.

Harry's head was spinning. Clutching at the red-tinged snow on the tree-trunk, his grip tightened as he heard the periodic yet mercifully fading booms in the distance. The pressure in his chest had been with him for most of the retreat. His lungs had, at times, threatened to betray him to the enemy, but the adrenalin reinforcements had answered his bugle call. It was only now that Harry felt a yawn of a more comforting kind. He closed his eyes and imagined a dark chasm beckoning him:

Go on, Harry, jump! You'll be safe in here. No more bright lights; no more orders; just peace...and warmth. You're feeling quite warm already, aren't you? Why don't you lie down? Take it easy. You've earned your stripes. They won't find you now, you know: too busy saving their own *skins.*

Harry opened his eyes and saw his breath ascending to form mini-clouds in the heavens. The trees were soberly renewing their sentry duties. He knew what he had to do. With one last effort, he tore off the three chevrons and smiled.

Death was inevitable: the war was lost.

One Good Turn
By
Mary Belfield

"Where have you been, gallivanting all day?"
She chirped at her Partner in her 'fishwife' way.
"I've fed the kids and cleaned out our home
With no help from you but all on my own.
Your family called round and asked for you
But finding you gone again, off they flew.

"I'm so sorry dear I got carried away
By the wonderful thermals out over the bay.
The sky was so blue and the sunshine was warm
The fish were abundant and the water so calm."
I truly meant to be back before now
I didn't want to cause a row."

"Well flap your wings and fly away
You can please yourself all night and day.
Find yourself another nest
All of us think that this is best.
The chicks and I now love your brother
For …One good turn deserves another!"

The Eye Of The Dragon
By
Jane Croft

Death is the ultimate paradox. It is the only certainty of life and yet it is unknowable. One must therefore be prepared for all eventualities. My master, the Son of Heaven, Emperor Qin Shi Huang, understood this as well as anyone. Thus it was that early in his reign he began to prepare for that last dreaded journey, and summoned the royal geomancers that he might consult them about the site for his mausoleum. At the same time he held out the hope of cheating death. To this end he expended great efforts in seeking the elixir of eternal life, sending forth his agents to search the known world. I, Lhao Tzu, was one. I will not enumerate all the adventures that befell me in that quest. I will relate only one, that by which I was both blessed and cursed.

One day, while travelling through a wild and remote valley, I saw a man lying by the roadside. At first I thought he was dead but as I approached I heard him groan. Hastening closer I saw that his clothing was torn and dirty, his grey hair and beard matted with blood from several deep wounds. I carried him into the shade beneath a tree and there gave him water from my own bottle. It revived him somewhat and he began to show awareness of his surroundings once more. As he did so, his eyes widened in sudden fear.

'My staff! Where is it?'

I looked around and saw a stout wooden stave lying in the road some yards away.

'It is yonder,' I replied.

'Bring it here, young man, I beg you.'

I nodded and obeyed. He closed one gnarled hand around it and an expression of relief appeared on his face.

'It is well,' he said.

In truth he looked so pale and ill and the injuries to his head so dire that I could scarcely see how the staff was going to be much good to him.

'You must rest, sir,' I told him. 'You surely cannot walk even with that to support you.'

'I have no time.' His breathing was laboured, his hands fumbling with the staff. 'Help me.'

'What must I do?'

'Take the end. That's it. Now unscrew it.'

I frowned for I could see no join, no sign that the top could in any way be separated from the rest. I suspected that his mind was addled by the blows he had received.

'Make haste. There is little time.' His tone was more desperate, more compelling.

So to humour him I grasped the top of the stave and twisted. To my amazement the upper section turned and began to part from the main stem. A few moments more and it separated completely to reveal a hollow compartment within. A glance revealed a scroll concealed there.

'Take out what you see,' he commanded.

Again I obeyed.

He nodded. 'This is what the robber was after, and what he must not be allowed to find.'

'What is it?' I asked.

'Open it.'

The scroll proved to be a map, beautifully drawn, and around the edges were written ancient characters in elegant calligraphy. My curiosity awakened.

'May I ask what this means?'

'No time now.' His breathing grew more laboured as though every breath were an effort. 'You must take this to Qin Shi Huang and tell him that it came to you from the hand of Sun Zheng.'

'Sun Zheng, the geomancer?'

'He.'

My amazement was total for who in all of China had not heard of the mystical powers of Sun Zheng? However, I had no space to indulge my astonishment for his expression grew more urgent.

'The man who attacked me was an agent of the warlord Deng Xao who has long sought the map for his own evil purposes. He would have no hesitation in selling this to the Emperor's enemies.'

Hearing that name I understood the old man's anxiety. Deng Xao had an insatiable craving for gold, and possession of the map would make him wealthy beyond the dreams of avarice.

'I will do all in my power to prevent the map falling into Xao's hands,' I replied.

'You must give it directly into the Emperor's hand.' Sun Zheng paused for breath. 'Tell him… that the gate to eternity is found… in the eye of the dragon.'

With that he fell silent. Sun Zheng was gone. For a moment I debated with myself what to do. Then it occurred to me that the agent who had attacked the old man might still be lurking in the vicinity, and thus I cast anxious looks around. However, there was no sign of movement anywhere. Deciding that I could not stop to examine the map more closely here I swiftly restored it to its hiding place and replaced the top of the stave. The join was so cunningly wrought that the surface of the wood revealed no trace of it. Then I covered the old man's body with stones to protect it from wolves and buzzards. It was a rude grave but the best that could be managed under the circumstances. Having laid Sun Zheng to rest, I took up his staff and continued on my way.

That evening I found a small cave and stopped to rest. It was dark and cold but prudence cautioned against lighting a fire for I could not be sure who might see it and come to investigate. Thus it was not until dawn next day that I had the opportunity to study the map once more.

The chart showed part of Shaanxi Province. Xian was clearly marked. However, it was not the location of the town that set my heart beating faster but the area bounded by Lishan Mountain and the Wei River. There the lay of the land was shaped like a dragon. My throat dried as Sun Zheng's words returned: *"...the gate to eternity is found in the eye of the dragon."* What could it mean? I searched the writing for further clues but what I read seemed to make little sense: "In the fire of the dragon's breath shall the human clay be restored. Thus shall man achieve immortality." I pondered this for some time but found no enlightenment. It came to me then that the only way to discover what it might mean was to go there and investigate. Accordingly I set out for Xian.

It was a journey of several days and as it continued I became increasingly certain that I was being followed. I had no physical evidence for this; in spite of my vigilance I could detect no sight or sound of pursuit. All I had to go on was instinct, a prickling at the back of my neck, but over the years I have learned to trust it and it has saved my life on several occasions. I felt equally certain that the unseen follower had also attacked Sun Zheng, and I was resolved not to be taken unawares. In a fair and open fight I was confident of giving a good account of myself for my training in the martial arts had been thorough. An ambush was something else though and must be avoided at all costs.

In the event, I reached my destination without incident. To better understand the map I climbed a hill that I might have a panoramic view. Then I studied the chart again. Using its points of reference I worked out roughly where the eye of the dragon was located. However, by that reckoning his breath was in a solid wall of rock. Knowing my calculations were imprecise I descended the hill and, on reaching the cliff, followed it for some distance. At length I came to the mouth of a cave. It was quite large and went back a long way, narrowing as it did so and finally disappearing into darkness. Taking a firm hold on my staff I ventured in.

Daylight penetrated for some distance but gradually the way grew darker and I had no means of illumination. Keeping my free hand on the rocky wall I took short and tentative steps forward. As I went deeper within silence and blackness thickened but, instead of the anticipated cold, the air grew warmer. It smelled of dust and age and something else that defied precise definition. It was madness to continue and yet I could not turn back. Time lost all meaning. Reality had been suspended save for my quiet footfalls and the sound of each indrawn breath, and truly I felt as though I had been swallowed alive in the dragon's maw.

I do not know how far I went before I realised that the darkness was becoming lighter. Gradually my eyes made out the walls and roof of the tunnel in which I stood. Wide enough for two men to pass side by side and higher than my head by about a yard, it was illuminated by a weird reddish glow emanating from myriad crystals in the rocky face. A few feet further on the passage ended in a great cavern. It too was filled with the eerie light by which I could make out its walls and in the midst a dark pit from which emanated wreaths of sulphurous vapour. The roof of the cavern was so high I could not discern it and stood gazing upwards in awestruck wonder.

It was then I heard a sound from the passage without; the soft scuffing sound of leather on stone. My pursuer had not been imagined. Flattening myself against the wall of the cavern I listened intently, straining to catch the least sound. The passage was silent but the prickling sensation at the back of my neck only intensified. Gripping the stave tighter I waited, scarcely daring to breathe.

A dark clad figure appeared at the entrance to the cavern. For a moment he paused then took a pace forward. Without waiting for more I launched myself at him, thrusting the end of the stave into his ribs. I heard him grunt and fall but he rolled and came to his feet. In his hand was a dagger, its blade glinting red like the eyes above the dark cloth that covered the lower part of his face. As he lunged I side-stepped and caught him another blow, but still he came on. The fight was short and savage with never a word exchanged. The world was reduced to flying feet and fists, the whirling stave and the slashing knife. Then the stave caught him across the knee and he staggered. The next blow brought him down. I heard the knife clatter on rock. Lifting the stave high I made to finish him but at that moment the floor shook and a mighty subterranean roar arose from the void with a cloud of yellow smoke. The sides of the pit so dark before began to glow red.

In terror I fled the cavern, running back along the tunnel, followed as it seemed by the roaring monster from the pit. A wave of heat gushed from the cavern's mouth and I darted a glance over my shoulder in time to see a huge pillar of fire shoot upwards from the void. Every crystal in the rock glowed blood red. The glow intensified until the walls and floor were dyed scarlet and the very air pulsed with a strange and powerful energy. Involuntarily I flung up an arm to shield my eyes and turned away. From the cavern behind me I heard a human scream of pure terror.

And then, as suddenly as it had come, the pillar of fire receded leaving behind a cloud of foul vapours, and the bloody light dimmed to a sullen glow. With infinite caution I looked around. The cavern was silent. The bare skin of my hands and face tingled with residual energy. Retrieving the fallen stave I crept back towards the cavern, half fearful of attack. None came. My mysterious assailant was lying on the rock floor quite still. Suspecting some trick I prodded the body with the end of the staff. What it met was not soft flesh. In disbelief I ventured closer and bent to touch. Then hand and mind recoiled together. The form, though perfect in every detail, was a man no longer but a figure of stone.

For a moment I could scarcely assimilate what my senses were telling me and so I touched the body again. This time there was no doubt. Nearby lay the assassin's blade, apparently untouched. I retrieved it. Then, taking a last glance around, I departed for the cave mouth once more. The relief afforded by fresh air and sunlight was enormous and I sank trembling against a rock giving thanks for the narrowness of my escape. When I felt calmer I examined the dagger; it was a fine weapon, beautifully balanced with an edge that would split a hair. The device on the hilt revealed that its owner had been a follower of the Hong, a cult of assassins who sold their skills for gold. Only the wealthiest could afford their services; men like Deng Xao for instance. At this realisation I saw my duty clearly: I must return to the Emperor and tell him all that he might best decide what to do.

Qin Shi Huang listened with close attention and growing wonder to the tale I related, his excitement almost palpable.

'Show us the map,' he said then.

I handed it to him and he unrolled the scroll, poring over it. Qin Shi Huang was then in his prime. Though only of average height, his was a warrior's strength. His bearded face was not handsome but it had a certain gravitas, enhanced by the aura of power he wore as effortlessly as his sumptuous silken robes.

'You have done well,' he continued, 'though we are saddened to learn of Sun Zheng's death for he was foremost among geomancers.'

I inclined my head respectfully but remained silent. The Emperor's expression grew thoughtful.

'Did the assassin speak before he died?'

'No, Highness. The only evidence of his identity was the costume I described and this dagger.'

He examined the weapon and then nodded. 'This is indeed the mark of the Hong. Of all our enemies only Deng Xao has the power now to work against us in this way.'

This was true. In his determination to unify China Qin Shi Huang had prosecuted his wars with ferocity and determination. One by one the states of Han and Zhao, Wei, Chu, Yan and Qi had fallen to his power, their leaders dead or subdued. Only Deng Xao remained unbowed.

'We shall deal with the problem in due course. Deng Xao shall be repaid for his treachery.' The Emperor regarded me steadily. 'We also reward those who serve us well. Yours shall be wealth and land as well as the position of a trusted adviser.'

I managed to stammer out my thanks for in truth I was overwhelmed. However, there was little time then to dwell on my sudden rise in the world for the Emperor turned again to the map. When he looked up his eyes glittered with satisfaction.

'We shall also give orders for the commencement of work on the royal mausoleum, according to the instructions given to us by the chart.' He read aloud: ' "The gate to eternity is found in the eye of the dragon.." There shall our tomb be constructed.'

So it was that the work on the great mausoleum was begun, a city of the dead that was to contain everything their royal master might need for his journey into the next life. I was charged with overseeing the work and with sending my master reports on its progress. From time to time Qin Shi Huang visited the site himself and each time he seemed well satisfied with what he saw. Then one day he took me aside.

'We desire that you show us the cave of the dragon's breath.'

I was not eager to return but, since even the smallest desire of an emperor is a command, we set out accompanied by a small detachment of armed guards. When we reached the mouth of the outer cave my master bade two of the soldiers accompany us. The rest were to remain behind. Then we went in. This time our progress was quicker for we had lighted torches to show the way, and we reached the inner cavern without difficulty. The Emperor looked about in wonder. The petrified body of the assassin was where I had left it and he examined it closely. Then he straightened. I saw him glance towards the guards and then towards the pit, his expression speculative.

'We shall try the truth of this matter,' he said then.

My gut tightened and I knew a moment of dread. Taking one of the lighted brands he commanded the guards to remain within the chamber while he and I walked aside for private speech. We retired some way into the passage.

'Now,' he said, 'we shall see if the dragon wakes.'

We didn't have long to find out. The screams of the two guards were terrible to hear. They haunt me still. Qin Shi Huang regarded the petrified forms with awe and then satisfaction as though the answer to some inner question had just been answered. He did not share his thoughts with me and presently we returned to the cave entrance in silence. Noting the absence of their two comrades the waiting guards exchanged glances but none dared to question the Emperor, and remounting the horses we returned to the construction site.

Nothing more was said about what had passed in the cave. In any case I was kept busy with my work and the Emperor with preparing his troops for war with Deng Xao. Within months a vast host was arrayed and ready to march. I did not witness the battle though from the accounts afterwards it was a swift and decisive victory for the Emperor. He had given orders that Deng Xao was to be taken alive. Unusually his men were also commanded to take as many prisoners as possible. In the end there were over seven thousand of them. In addition the Emperor's troops took much booty: hundreds of bronze war chariots, fine horses and many thousands of weapons – swords, spears and crossbows. At that time there was much speculation as to the probable fate of the prisoners for Qin Shi Huang was renowned as a fierce and ruthless opponent in war. It was widely believed that he intended to make an example of them and thus snuff out any remaining fires of rebellion among the lesser warlords. However, the Emperor kept his own counsel on the matter.

To the general surprise the captives were chained and brought to a camp near the construction site, along with the captured booty. Then they were set to work to dig a great pit, 250 yards long, 68 yards wide and 16 feet deep. Every three yards it was divided by a puddle wall fortified with wooden columns, earth and reeds. The floor was lined with black brick. The pit was not on the original plans but my polite inquiry elicited only an enigmatic smile and the injunction to be patient.

Patience was indeed required for the work took some years to complete. During this time the prisoners of war were treated surprisingly well, given better rations than the rest of the labourers and beaten only in exceptional circumstances so that very few died. When their task was done the captives were taken aside and ordered to put on their battle robes and armour, an instruction received with surprise and disbelief but obeyed nonetheless. Then they were formed up, chained once more and marched away towards the south. I was not to see them again for some time.

Then, one morning, two months later, the Emperor summoned me to his presence and bade me accompany him.

'For today, Lhao Tzu, we shall divulge the purpose of the great pit.'

I professed myself delighted. In truth my curiosity made it hard to restrain the many queries that rose to my lips. However, the Emperor's will permits of no question and thus I accompanied him in obedient silence.

When we reached the place all the words I would have uttered withered away and I could only stand and stare. The pit was no longer empty. Beneath my startled gaze stood an army; row upon row of armed warriors, columns of foot soldiers alternated with bronze war chariots drawn by teams of proud horses, in a company seven thousand strong. No sound or movement issued from that great host. All were locked in eerie silence. Beneath their stony gaze I felt all the hairs prickle on the back of my neck.

'In the fire of the dragon's breath shall the human clay be restored,' said the Emperor.

I turned to meet his gaze. My shock must have been evident for I saw him smile.

'Deng Xao and his army shall atone for their treason by guarding their Emperor in the afterlife.'

He sounded quite assured, but looking upon the massed ranks of clay warriors I could not share his confidence. Would they guard their Emperor in death, I wondered, or would they rise up again and be avenged?

That night sleep eluded me for my mind was crowded with troubled thoughts. Every time I closed my eyes I saw the silent warriors and felt the weight of their gaze upon me. I could hear their dying screams. A thousand times I wished I had never discovered that dreadful cavern, or having discovered it that I had never imparted its secret. No amount of remorse now could absolve me for having done so. Men perish every day; war, famine, pestilence and old age account for us all. Until then I had not feared death, only considered it a distant inevitability. Now the afterlife seemed much closer. And when I made the final journey through that dreaded portal, what would lie beyond? Then my mind returned to that silent waiting host and I shivered.

The Witching Owl
By
Claire Walker

The scratching noise woke Billy again, and he reached for the bedside light. As the dim glow filled the room, his left eye twitched. His eyes scanned the area but saw nothing. Quickly, he lit a cigarette. He flicked his tab end into the full ashtray. His mother would be disgusted at him for smoking in bed.

Flinging the covers off his bed, he walked over to the living area of his student flat. The room smelt stale, so he opened a window. He craned his neck out. Revellers spilled out of bars, and Billy wondered if it was too late to go out. He sat down at his desk, and looked at the law journal. It had been open at the same page for weeks now.

He scanned the pages of the local newspaper, whilst lighting another cigarette. A macabre picture of an owl caught his attention, and he read the accompanying article.

> The Witching Owl is a small, sprightly beast, similar in size to a weasel. With sharp teeth and white feathers, its large, orange eyes search for prey, as its head rotates 360°. At moonlight, one could easily mistake the bird for a snowy owl, but this creature is not likely to be found on the pages of a *Harry Potter* novel.

He was about to throw the newspaper in the bin, when he caught sight of his home town in the article. He read on.

> Folklore has it that this beast was created by witches in the twelfth Century. William Brown, local woodsman, caught a witch stealing his tools. With the aide of fellow workers, he tied her up and set fire to her against a felled tree. The following day, the witches came in search of their friend, and found her charred remains.
>
> The witches were unable to catch William, who was forever guarded by his woodsmen. Some weeks later, the witches decided upon supernatural methods for retribution. The woodsmen came across them in the woods.

Billy smiled at the drawing of a cauldron, before continuing.

> The witches threw a concoction of livestock, such as owls, weasels and ferrets into a steaming pot. They chanted and cackled over it. The forest echoed with the howls of animals being boiled alive.
>
> Out of the bubbling, steaming brew rose a devilish creature. The woodsmen could just make out the witches' mantra. They heard the words, *Witching Owl, Kill William Brown, Eat him, Beat him, Bring him* ...The witches didn't finish their spell, as the woodsmen set to them with their axes.
>
> The recent killings of local livestock just last month, and sightings of what was thought to be a snowy owl, have resurrected the story. This is much to the amusement of local twitchers. While there is no evidence surrounding the Owl's existence, there have been a handful of sightings over the years, predominantly in the Derbyshire region. This gives us food for thought: Does the Witching Owl have some unfinished business?'

The Witching Owl

The hackles rose on Billy's neck. Absently rubbing the scar on his cheek, he remembered a story his mother told him.

Quickly, he picked up his mobile, and called home.

'Mum?'

'Billy, what's up? It's so late.'

Billy looked at his watch: 10:15pm.

'Sorry, Mum.'

'Are you all right?'

'Er … fine, thanks. Listen, do you remember that story you used to tell me … about me being attacked as a baby?'

'Oh, you always used to love me telling you that story. Men are fascinated by their own scars.' She chuckled, then re-counted the tale she had told him a hundred times.

'You were about a year old, it was a warm summer's evening in-'

'Yeah, okay Mum, just cut to the attack, will you?'

'I'll tell it how it is, Billy, or not at all!'

'Sorry, go on.'

'I'd left you sleeping in your cot in the bedroom, when I heard you cry.' She paused, actually enjoying telling the story, even some 19 years later.

'And?'

'Well, I couldn't believe my eyes. You were being set upon by this white, bird-rat thing. It looked evil. I pulled you away just before it was about to take a bite from you.'

Billy touched the scar on his face again.

'I clasped my arms tightly around you, and watched as this thing jumped high into the air, its sharp claws aiming towards us both. I was terrified.'

'Did it look like an owl?'

She ignored the question, carried away with the story. 'I put you in the wardrobe, grabbed your dad's cricket bat, and whacked it with all the force I could muster. White feathers flew everywhere.'

Billy shivered.

'I set to it again. It were whimpering at my feet when I knocked the life out of it.'

'What happened to it? Did you take it to the police?'

She laughed. 'What? No. We had to get you to hospital, you were hurt quite badly. That's how you got your scar.'

'What did you do with the ... er ... bird?'

'It stunk like hell in there, but we couldn't find it. It must have slunk off to the woods to die. Anyway, why do you ask?'

'Just curious, that's all. I read something-' Billy decided against continuing. His thoughts were irrational.

'Are you eating enough? It shouldn't be all parties, you know. How's the course going?'

'Yeah, yeah,' Billy was keen to avoid a lecture.

'Anyway, I'll do a roast on Sunday. Beef, your favourite.'

'Okay, Mum, I'll see you then.' Billy was about to put down the phone down, when he remembered something. 'Oh, Mum, just one thing. Dad has a smaller scar like mine too, but on the other side of his face.'

'Oh, yes, I suppose he has.'

'How did he get it?'

'Oh, love, I've no idea. Probably a cricket ball. Are you sure you're okay? You're not taking drugs, are you?'

'I'm fine, Mum. Ask Dad about the scar, will you?'

'He's in bed. You two can talk about your war wounds on Sunday.' She laughed as Billy ended the call.

Billy circled his desk twice before snatching away the seat. He opened his laptop and typed into the search engine ... *Witching Owl, Derbyshire*. He waited for the results to appear. Two hours later, with no further information than the magazine article provided, Billy slammed down the screen. Unsure whether he was angry from lack of information, or how much it had taken over his evening, he walked over to the window. He opened the window fully and stared into the night sky.

His fingers tingled with numbness and a prickling sensation stole under his skin. He watched the sky darken before him at an unnerving speed. It was as if someone had dimmed the city lights. When he looked down, it seemed like the pavement was rising towards the sky, towards *him*. Billy blinked and shook his fingers, but the itchiness now pulsed in his arms. He looked up again. In the distance, a flock of black crows approached. As they neared, their cries pierced the sky. None of the people in the street looked up and they seemed unaware of the moving pavement. Even in the dark, the crows cast shadows onto the street. Billy's breathing grew erratic, every other breath now a frightened pant. He looked away, then back again; reality did not return.

Then he saw it, leading the crows. The bird he had been frantically researching on the web. It approached at speed, reaching his window in seconds. Its wingspan filled Billy's view. The lights in his flat illuminated its white, matted feathers. Its mouth was a black orifice of sharp yellowing teeth, encrusted with flesh and blood.

The bird stopped and hovered at the window. Its orange eyes locked onto Billy's and held his stare. He was transfixed, until the bird suddenly swooped down and out of sight.

Billy leant over the window and had to physically stop himself from free-falling.

'What the hell … ?'

He rushed out of the door and down the communal stairs. Crashing open the exit to the street, the air was warm and still.

He raced around the streets, gasping and panting. Searching the sky, he saw nothing.

'Hey, watch out, man!'

Billy knocked into someone carrying a drink between bars. 'Sorry.' He hung his head, and slowly returned to his flat.

In the bathroom, he splashed cold water onto his face. He could still hear his heartbeat.

He had a fitful sleep that night. The scratching noise he had been hearing the last few weeks plagued him. It continued for days. Thoughts of the incident took over his every waking hour.

On Sunday, he had dinner at his parents' house. He realised he had barely eaten since he spoke to his mother last. He was ravenous, and listened to his mother as he enjoyed the beef, cooked rare as he liked it.

'You hungry, son?' she laughed, watching Billy suck on the

meat, the hot blood dripping down his throat.

His mind was still full of the Witching Owl. The redness trickled down his chin, and surrendering to his own thoughts, he pictured the creature, its teeth stained with blood and flesh.

As his mother continued to talk, Billy's attention was caught by something at the open window.

His father followed his glare.

'What's up, son?' he asked.

Billy was lost in macabre thoughts of flying into the air. He saw himself grabbing his parents' heads and smashing them together. The sound of skulls crushing and the deathly screams fed his energy. His strength was insurmountable. He would tear at their necks with his fingernails. Flesh and blood flying across the room as his hands tore at their bodies. It would take just seconds to pulverise them. He suddenly saw himself feasting on their organs.

Billy shivered as he came to, grappling with the horrific thoughts that had just flashed through his mind. He stared down at his beef. He was embarrassed to catch his parent's gaze.

Realising his mum had stopped talking, Billy cleared his throat, about to talk about University. It was then that he finally looked up.

Billy gasped, the bile rising instantly. Vomit escaped out of his mouth and down his nostrils. The mutilated bodies of his parents lay in front of him. They were barely recognisable.

'Ha … Have I done this?'

He stood over them, hot tears flowing down his face. Shaking his head, and trying to stop the nausea, he clamped his hand over his mouth.

Just as he buckled at the knees, an icy wind brought the Witching Owl itself through the window. Billy turned, his eyes locking onto the animal's. It lunged forward and reached his neck. Death came quickly; a deep incision to his throat slitting the carotid and jugular. For Billy, it was a welcome release from the scene he had just witnessed. For the Witching Owl, it was the finish of something it had started some 900 years earlier.

***

The yellow tape surrounding the small bungalow wafted in the breeze. Camera crews and reporters filled the tiny front garden.

'This local community is stunned and devastated in the aftermath of the heinous murders of William and Mary Brown, along with their son, William. A local joiner, William Brown was well loved in the neighbourhood. Mary was a warden at the local church. William, their only son, just twenty years old, had begun a law degree at Sheffield University. The area has been cordoned off and a search started some three hours ago.'

The cameraman zoomed into the windows of the bungalow and then the forest behind it.

The Witching Owl was perched on a branch, its claws thick with flesh. Human blood oozed off its tongue.

Suddenly, it opened its wings and tucking its feet into its body, soared deep into the forest.

'What the hell was that?' The cameraman yelled, as others stared into the sky.

'Was that an Owl?' the reporter asked, walking towards him.

The cameraman shivered. 'I don't know.' Suddenly, he turned around.

'Did you hear that?'

'What?'

'That chanting?' He pointed to the woods behind.

'No. Bill, are you okay?'

Bill Brown gulped. Out of the corner of his eye, he saw a flock of crows approaching.

Echoes
By
Jane Croft

The past's another country,
And the place that she would be:
The present has no meaning
That her aged eyes can see.

The rhythm of a distant waltz
Plays softly sweet and clear,
And she dances to the music
That only she can hear

And echoes of a much-loved voice
From sixty years away
Give back the words he spoke to her
As it were yesterday:

'Take this likeness, darling,
And wear it next your heart:
Then I'll be with you always,
Though for this time we part.

The bugles bid us march
Toward the din of fight,
And duty bids us strive
For freedom and the right.

And should I ne'er return,
And you know grief and pain,
I'll be with you always,
Until we meet again.

Destiny's uncertain,
The future's out of sight,
So, darling, hold me close
And dance with me tonight.'

The guns have long been silent,
And the myriad years have sped,
But he lives on in memory
With the music in her head.

Her frail old eyes look inward
Through the dreaming twilight air,
To the ballroom and the dancers,
And the soldier waiting there.

The shadows hold no terrors,
Nor the fading of the light,
For she'll be with her darling,
And she'll dance with him tonight.

Bitter Sweets
by
Claire Walker

Tom drives the *Sweetie Train* at Draythorpe on the East Coast. It chugs up and down the sea front every few minutes. It passes the bright arcade lights and tiresome jingles on one journey, returning on the coast side, where the tide always seems a mile out.

Tom doesn't smell the chips soaked in vinegar. Having chain-smoked *Park Drive* cigarettes throughout his youth, his sense of smell is weak. But he *can* smell the holidaymakers. They come in droves, like refugees stowed away on a long distance lorry, spewing out onto the littered streets.

It's raining today and there is no seaside cheer. The surly passengers greet Tom as if *he's* responsible for the weather. No one makes eye contact as they squeeze their chip butty arses onto the small wooden benches.

There are fewer people on the streets today, but there is still a queue. It's Tom's fault that some have to wait five minutes for the next train. Stressful sighs are reminiscent of a commuter at Kings Cross, rather than a tourist filling his time between stuffing a machine with coins, or his mouth with fried donuts.

Tom collects fares and locks the carriages, something he's done a million times over. The rain washes off his umbrella onto his polyester uniform.

'Do we get a sweetie *now*?' a woman snaps, handing over

her fare, and pointing to the sign advertising "free sweet for children".

'It's called the *Sweetie Train*,' Tom says, no emotion in his voice.

The woman nudges her husband, and whispers, 'What does that mean?'

Tom wonders if she'd be so keen to thrust a sweet down her kid's throat, if she knew it was years out of date, and laced with Warfarin.

Of course, the sweets are fine; it just amuses him to think that way. He takes a slow walk beside the train, handing out sweets, before climbing into the driving seat.

He pulls the chord to sound the horn, and calls, 'Hold on tight.' It would have been reciprocated with a cheer had the sun been shining.

He accelerates as he approaches the first speed bump, letting out a macabre laugh as each carriage jolts, and loose paintwork drops onto his trousers.

The train takes fares of over £300 an hour; a tin of paint costs just ten pounds. He cannot remember the last time it was so much as serviced.

Tom knows about profit, having been an Accounts Clerk in a former life, where double entry book-keeping was his forte. He enjoyed nothing more than slowly filling out the columns in leather-bound ledgers. If his life had balanced like his numbers, he'd be sunning himself in Marbella right now, rather than driving a hairdryer up and down the sea front.

At the mini roundabout on the High Street, Tom increases his speed for sheer amusement, and steers head on into the bend. His concentration slips for a moment just as a pensioner walks straight into the road without looking. Tom swerves, causing the second carriage to veer off to the right. This has a chain effect on the ones behind it, and the third carriage skids, turning 180°, crashing into a bollard. Moans are quickly replaced with frightened screams. Passengers try to jump out, but the carriages fall like dominoes, the last two slamming into the back of the ones in front. The back section ricochets and breaks off, picking up speed and veering towards an embankment. Protected only by wooden fencing and rocks, there's a twenty foot fall beyond. Scrabbling limbs and children's cries burst out of the faded yellow cart.

Tom pictures it crashing onto tourists making sandcastles on the beach.

Of course, he imagines it, as this whole scenario happens only in his mind; a sick action-replay to get him through the hours. Tom knows that such a crash would be impossible for a train that barely reaches 10 miles an hour.

He stops at the Pier and listens to the groans of, 'Two quid for that! What a bloody rip off.'

He watches the passengers embark, lighting up another cheap cigarette. He does not see the pool of petrol spilling from the train, trailing at his feet. Inhaling the fag deeply, he looks up to see the sun forcing its way through the clouds. The nicotine fills the gaps in his soul.

It is time for the return journey. Tom looks down as he flicks his half-smoked cigarette to the ground. Too late, he notices the rainbow of colours reflected in the petrol slick.

The blast is immediate, engulfing him within seconds. This time, Tom hears for real the screams he imagined just moments ago.

The flames forage rapidly on his skin; he does not fight them. All the passengers are now off the carriages and their wild eyes glare at the blaze from a safe distance.

Fire rips through the small tourist train, and the intense heat burns blue on the old wooden frames. Swirls of grey and black smoke twist and meander upwards.

The sound of sirens pierce the smoke-filled sky, and Tom pictures himself handing out sweets, his face scarred and twisted. Determined not to read the headlines through bandages tomorrow, he moves closer into the burning carriage. One intake of breath and it's the end of the line for Tom. The pain is intense but not as prolonged as the daily anguish he feels.

The dark figure in the centre of the flames diminishes rapidly as the fire eats him.

The Three Rs
By
Carol Vardy

Liam, Isaac and Justin, known to their friends as Rooney, Renaldo and Rio, were keen Manchester United fans. They looked forward to their Friday football lesson. Rio and Renaldo were brothers; Rooney was their cousin. They would only wear red and white football gear.

Above the screaming, yelling, and general noise made by the excited boys and hysterical girls who stayed behind to watch, one voice screeched above the rest.

'Ronaldo, quick now; pass the ball this way. Come on, stop messing about,' Rooney snarled. 'What a rubbish game.'

There was no action today. He liked to be goalie like Van der Sar. He was also a fan of Rooney and it was easier for his pals to shout. The thrill he got when he dived for the ball, the praise on a good catch. Everybody patted him on the back and cheered him. He rolled about on the ground. Being covered in mud didn't worry him; he never even noticed it. But today the game was going nowhere so he amused himself by kicking the wet grass, flicking clods of soil into the air. Then he tried to catch them.

Rio yelled to Ronaldo, 'Kick it or I'll get you later!'

Ronaldo poked his tongue out at him and then gave the ball such a punt it flew through the air at high speed. Unfortunately, at the same time, Rooney let out an enormous yawn which stretched his mouth wide. The ball arrived at such speed it hit him full in the face and knocked him flat on his back. As he lay screaming from shock and pain, his mother ran over from the sidelines.

'Oh Liam,' she sobbed. 'I told you football was a dangerous game.'

She wrapped her arms about him, checking to see if his nose was broken. Rooney felt only embarrassment and tried to push her away.

'Mum, stop it, I'm okay,' he panted, and struggled to get out of her grasp so that he could stand up.

The mothers of the young footballers were all huddled together, thankful that it wasn't raining heavily. They dreaded washing the young footballers' muddy clothes, even though they took it in turns. As they chatted and laughed, the sudden scream stopped all conversation. They hoped it wasn't from their child. The referee blew his whistle. He felt sorry for Rooney. As he was an only child his mum did tend to fuss. He'd noticed how keen a player the lad was; after school he would throw down his school bag to use as a goal post. There was always someone ready to kick a ball with him.

'Liam,' she said.

'Mum, it's Rooney,' he whispered.

'Oh all right,' she said as she patted his head and stroked stray hairs off his face. 'Come on, we'll go straight home. You poor baby.'

'I want to go with the others, please Mum.' He felt so embarrassed and looked imploringly at the ref.

'He'll be alright, Gaynor. The lad's just taken a bit of a knock. He'll probably have a black eye tomorrow.'

Rooney had been friends with Renaldo and Rio since infant school. He often played rough and tumble with them, so he wasn't going to let this stop him from playing football.

The boys changed out of their mud-splattered clothes, amid lots of chattering, pushing and loud laughter. The game had given them an appetite, so as usual they tucked into sausage and chips at the local café.

The Three R's

After getting good exam results at school, the three boys transferred to a college that specialised in their chosen subject. An invitation arrived. Their old school was having a reunion so Gaynor rang Liam and he arranged for himself and his two close friends to be there. It would be good seeing everyone after all these years.

Shaking hands with their old teachers and friends, it seemed like only yesterday that they'd played football together. The girls giggled and fluttered their eye lashers at them and queued up for their autographs. The old head master, who had recently taken retirement, cleared his throat. After he'd welcomed everyone he asked the three smartly dressed young men to come onto the stage.

'Your parents must be very proud of you,' he enthused, 'and pleased to see not a scrap of mud in sight.'

Everyone who knew the boys laughed at this.

The head continued, 'Liam, Isaac and Justin have been given the honour of being chosen to represent our town when we play against Manchester United.' Thunderous applause followed, whooping and cheering resounding around the hall. 'We are thrilled and delighted and they have agreed to perform for us this evening. I proudly present, 'The Three R's'

The pianist began to play. The three young football lovers had chosen to attend Music College and now their fantastic voices were heard all over the world. The song they were about to sing was 'Abide with me.' They still followed 'Man U' but they also supported their own town.

Memory of the Rock
By
Sue Pacey

It was a distressing sight seeing Pat O'Cleary weep, even for his wife. For he was a big man and you didn't expect it.

Pat could first remember crying when he was six, when his dad had fallen beneath the farm's heavy tractor back in Sligo.

Keep clear of un-propped body. The warning had been scratched and encrusted with dirt, but was still readable. That was, of course, assuming Patrick O'Cleary senior *could* read. He had been thirty-one.

"You wanna' talk Pat?"

"In a minute, babe."

He pulled off his sweat-stained shirt and blew his nose loudly on it, before throwing it in the corner of the bedroom. He sat heavily on the bed.

Lucy moved over from where she had been watching by the door to gently massage the back of his neck.

"Can I get you anything, darling?"

"A large Bushmills thanks."

"I'll get the bottle." Lucy picked up the discarded shirt with its distinctive white lettering – **Yorkshire Cave Rescue** – and took it downstairs for washing. She knew by her own instinct and from her husband's demeanour that the outcome of this particular incident had been less than favourable. Her man rarely cried. She had only ever seen him weep twice.

The first time was on their wedding day when she had walked down the aisle of the little country church, high on the hill overlooking Kinsale. She had felt like a princess, on her father's arm for the last time, and, only a short walk away from her future husband. She had turned to him and lifted her veil, revealing a row of pink and peach rosebuds in her raven-black hair - and big Pat O'Cleary had wept like a child at her beauty. The perfume from her bouquet seemed to surround the pair with all the ancient symbolism she had intended for the occasion. Roses for love, sweet lavender and thyme for protection and yew for longevity.

None of this was lost on Pat, who stood in adoration, until the priest uttered the time-honoured words "Dearly beloved."

The words of Grandmother Philomena echoed in her head. "Ah, 'tis only a *real* man who can cry at the beauty of a May bride, so it is."

The only other time she had seen her husband cry was when their daughter had been thrust squalling into the world, as if angry at the journey. The baby had been handed pink and unwashed to her father, and as she gazed at him through vernix-coated lids, Pat had fallen in love all over again.

The cornflower-blue eyes like her Mamma's seemed to say, "Well Papa, I'm here, so love me unconditionally." Pat's heart had melted like snow in June and the tears flowed once more.

And that, thought Lucy, *had been that. Until now.*

Handing him a glass, she poured a generous slug of Bushmills, setting down the bottle within reach on the bedside table. She sat on the bed and patted the quilt in invitation. But Pat did not sit. He stood, gazing out of the huge window which overlooked the Yorkshire hills; his eyes still glassy.

"I told a lie today, babe."

"Why?"

"It was the proverbial line of least resistance - and it was a huge, deliberate lie. A mega lie...a whopper. It was the biggest lie in the world and I'll probably go straight to hell!"

Lucy sat silent, expressionless, waiting until he found his time. Presently, he turned whisky in hand. It was the moment of confession – the opening of the door; the sitting, head bowed in penitence by the grill.

Bless me father, for I have sinned. It is twelve years since my last confession.

Better late than never! Pat could hear the Sligo lilt of Father Ryan's voice, his least-deaf ear inclined toward the pierced metal grill. *What is your sin, my son?*

Pat sipped the fierce amber liquid and sighed deeply, thinking of home.

For Ireland was *still* home and, lovely though this part of Yorkshire was, Pat's heart would always belong to the 'old country'. In Co. Sligo, the land was king.

Whilst some farmed and others climbed in the Ballygawley mountains, Pat preferred to burrow into the sweet, rocky earth, beneath; a caver, like his brothers from an early age. In that secret, silent world where few were privileged to venture could be found water so pure it was like looking through glass. There had always been something magical about disappearing into the earth to discover a new cave, cool and pristine. Moving down, safely roped, to see rock formations dripping with water, Pat would marvel at untouched beauty. Stalactites and stalagmites, which had taken millennia to form, reaching their bony fingers towards each other, brought a lump to his throat each time he saw them.

And always, the echo of Grandfather Sean Patrick's voice. "Remember boy...that tites come down!" And the wicked twinkle in the old man's eyes as he said it.

Then, there came a whole new world. To Dublin – and medical school – where Pat had come to understand that life was not so simple. He saw everything that the human condition could throw; from the most heroic bravery to the raw savagery inflicted on his fellow man. And he had learned to deal with it, returning to the world beneath the earth's surface, whenever he could.

A quiet, thoughtful man, Pat preferred his patients to be asleep and had found his niche in anaesthetics. This had brought the family to Yorkshire where he was Senior Registrar in nearby Pickering. The job was good; just one step down from a consultancy- and therefore, only two steps down from God himself!

Pete Greene – known affectionately as 'the mole' - could hardly believe his luck. He had led the local cave-rescue- all volunteers – for twenty years and had never had the luxury of a permanent doctor *and* a 'gas man' no less, experienced, willing *and* living on the doorstep!

"Don't you ever bloody well contemplate shoving off back to Paddy-land!" he would tell Pat at least once a month. "You were sent from heaven."

There was no danger, however, of Pat deserting, at least for the foreseeable future. He loved the area and his family was settled and their number was about to be increased to four in the next couple of weeks.

At last, he turned and walked over to where Lucy was sitting on the bed and sank down beside her. One arm settled around her shoulders; the fingers of the other carelessly caressing the swollen belly which nurtured their son.

"Was it bad, Pat?"

"Yes, very bad." The baby kicked vigorously and he smiled, despite himself.

"You ready to talk yet, big man?"

"Yeah!"

Lucy passed him the bottle of Bushmills and he refilled his glass.

****

The shrill ring of the phone had disturbed the peace of a Sunday morning.

A couple of seconds later his 'beeper' had flashed and buzzed noisily into life; the 'belt and braces' approach that ensures all members of the rescue team can be contacted.

With a groan, Pat rolled out of bed and pulled on his pants. He bent and kissed Lucy who smiled and turned over, snuggling beneath the quilt.

"Got to go, honey."

"Come back safe," she murmured automatically, not quite awake.

"Hi guys." Deputy leader, Mark Thomas' face wore a grave expression as he prepared for the briefing. He sat on a boulder. "What we've got here are a couple of experienced lads who set out early to climb Mattick Fell from the west. No problem there. For those of you not too familiar, the ridge leads to the entrance of the cave system at Sappa Gill. Apparently, just inside the entrance to the first descent, one guy slipped on a loose rock-pile. So, let's see what we have, shall we? Three teams of two. I'm leading today. Doc...You're in the second wave with Moley, okay?" Pat nodded his assent as they all began to re-check the safety equipment, and the team began the short but steep trek to the cave mouth.

The casualty was thirty feet below the main entrance and curiously well off to the left of the main angle of descent.

'Moley' Greene was puzzled. "How the hell did he get he manage to get so far off course? The natural way would have been to drop vertically and not off at an angle. Looks like the debris underfoot rolled him off to one side. I'll bet you couldn't duplicate this if you tried a thousand times."

The safety ropes that joined the two men together were still in place, but with enough slack for the other one to return to the surface to summon help.

Twenty-nine year old Simon Holloway was trapped up to his chest. The lower half of his body was wedged where he had fallen down a thin crevasse of solid rock. He was conscious, but in extreme pain. One arm and shoulder were obviously badly fractured and probably dislocated too, judging by the angle. There was a large laceration on his cheek which had been bleeding profusely and he was having difficulty breathing.

Pat crawled into the restricted space next to the man, swapping places with the caver who had been with him, to fix an oxygen mask. He talked, gently, in a practised fashion, assessing all the while. Simon Holloway's lips remained blue, even with the extra light the powerful LED lamp mounted on his helmet afforded.

"Simon, I'm going to fix a needle in your arm and give you a shot of morphine. Okay? It'll make you a bit more comfortable."

The young man nodded, his breathing a little easier. A wry smile crossed his lips. "Thanks."

As the drug took effect he became drowsy, his head to one side, resting on a small well-placed pillow. Pat spoke close to his ear. "Just going to the surface to muster the troops, then we'll see about getting you out of here." In response, came only the same wry smile and a wave of nausea rose in Pat's belly as he scrambled and hauled his way the thirty feet to the surface. He walked in silence to sit on an outcrop of rock a few feet away where the team waited with Simon Holloway's older brother.

"We came out early," began Don Holloway, "to get a start on Sappa Gill. I just don't know how it happened. We've done this cave dozens of times. Sappa's a tight bitch in places until you get down into the vault, but nothing we haven't done before. It was a bit slippery, but all the safety was in place. We aren't silly kids on a dare-devil jaunt. We've both been caving since we were teenagers." He looked up at the team who hadn't commented, reading their thoughts. "I know. There should always be four of us. Today though, the others went sick and we decided to go anyway." His gaze returned to the patch of ground between his feet.

Mac Jones placed a hand on his shoulder. "Don't beat yourself up mate...we've all done it at one time or another. Go back to your brother eh? We need Pete Greene back up here for a planning meeting so we can get cracking."

"Right Doc, so how do we play this?" 'Moley' Greene strode to join the group. "Sorry Mark, I know you're leading on this shout, but with such a badly injured casualty, I think we have to play it by the Doc's rules. So," he said turning to Pat, "how much muscle will we need to haul him out?"

Pat said nothing.

"Do we need the hydraulics?" Pat O' Cleary stared at the ground, his pulse racing.

"Pat...do we...?"

"I'm afraid it's not going to be as easy as that!" Pat stood to face them, his face expressionless. "There's no easy way of saying this, guys...so, listen up. This is the score." He paused and inhaled deeply. "Simon has fallen down a deep, narrow fissure in the rock and he went with rapid descent. That force crushed his pelvis inwards allowing him to fall up to his chest. The pelvic bones would have then sprung outwards again, trapping him fast. There is probably massive bleeding into his abdomen." He looked around at the faces of the rescue team. "The bottom line is, guys...he's not coming out of there."

****

Pat O'Cleary was sick to his stomach. He had just spent half an hour trying to contact the Orthopaedic consultant on call at York General hospital.

"Where's the feckin' bastard when you need him?" he raved, well away from the mouth of the cave. "Probably in bed with his feckin' fat wife, safe and warm under the quilt. Feck him!" Pete Greene placed a hand on his shoulder. Pat glared. "Five answer-phone messages. Five!" He stalked away to administer another large dose of morphine. This was not a decision he wanted to make now or ever, *and* certainly not alone.

Twenty minutes later, he got a reply.

Alexander Forde, Senior Trauma Consultant had uttered two words after Pat had finished talking. "Bloody Hell!" There followed a long silence. Pat could hear deep breathing and the older man lighting a cigarette. He coughed. "Okay Pat. Put the camera down...let's confirm it. I know you're sure, but let's do it anyway. Cover all the bases."

Pat shoved the mobile back in his hip pocket, cursing under his breath, trying to concoct a conversation with some hope in it. He was failing miserably.

The state of the art fibre-optic camera only confirmed what the team already knew, when they had eventually managed to manoeuvre it between rock and swollen flesh. The readings on the surface computer showed that if any attempt had been made to pull Simon Holloway out, they would, literally, have torn the young man in half. In a fit of paranoia, Pat had them check the results three times. He took out his mobile and dialled.

Alexander Forde's voice crackled in Pat's ear. "Then you have no choice my friend. You know what you must do, God help you." The line went dead.

"Feck you!" said Pat aloud and threw the phone as far as he could. "Pete, get his brother for me, will you please?"

****

Don Holloway was shaking.

"What are you saying Doc? That's my brother in there. Now let's just tie some more ropes around his body and haul him out for God's sake. What are we waiting for?"

Pat faced him, placing his huge hands on the man's shoulders. "Come on mate. Let's just you and me take a walk."

Grief and grim realisation must be allowed to run its course. There can be no shortcuts.

Half an hour later, Don Holloway had finally understood the mechanics on the third or fourth gentle explanation. That was, that there were thousands of tons of ancient, immovable rock encasing a man's body in a death grip. It was like the expandable coat hanger you hang trousers on...but in reverse. Don had sobbed, head in his hands. He had walked off and thumped the nearest rock, then stared into the distance whilst Pat waited quietly, facing his own demons. He had come back and asked meekly if the legs could be amputated. Pat merely shook his head sadly and Don answered his own question. "No, of course not. He's too far down. You can't cut a man off at the waist. So what is it to be? Do we wait for him to die? That's my brother in there!" His anguish spilled over into anger.

"No," said Pat simply; the quiet man, again in control.

"What then? Put him down like an injured dog?"

Pat did not answer. The silence was, nevertheless, affirmation.

"He mustn't know."

"He won't. I promise you."

"For God's sake! His girlfriend's due to have their first kid in four weeks time. How the hell am I supposed to tell her?"

A stab of pain shot through Pat's heart. He dared not allow himself to think of Lucy.

"Go back to your brother," he said simply, patting Don's shoulder.

Soon, they lay close to one another inside the cave, their faces almost touching. Don's breathing was synchronised with his brother's, as if willing a life and future into the young man. But, to his credit, he showed no hint of his pain or the coming end.

Bending over his rucksack, Pat prepared the injections. That bit was easy. The intra-venous line had already been sited for the morphine. There was no work to do really. No knocking up a vein to insert the cannula. No need to tape it in place. Sweat ran down his back. He wiped beads of it from his brow as it threatened to drip into his eyes. His hands shook as he tried to steady the syringe.

Shit! I'm about to kill a man.

No one looked at him. No one spoke – each cocooned with his own thoughts.

Pat took a deep breath and prepared to be lowered into the shaft. Mark Thomas knelt, eye to eye with him, his gaze steely. "Do this for him, the brother, that woman and the little baby," he said.

"I've never so much as squashed a spider, Mar, and I'm shitting myself," Pat whispered.

"He's relying on you and your expertise, mate."

"I know." And taking another deep breath, he nodded and let out the rope; the calm assured medic once again.

"Simon, here's what we're going to do. I'm going to put you under anaesthetic to allow all your muscles to relax completely. Then, when you're asleep, we're going to pull you out. We're all here with you, Simon. Don's here and there will be no pain. Are you ready?"

Simon's eyes flickered open and he nodded. Pat held his gaze, rock-steady.

"Do you understand Simon? No pain." He connected the first syringe.

"Simon nodded. There was that wry smile again. "Doc?"

"Yes mate?"

"Go and see my son for me?"

"You can go and see him for yourself very soon. Now, have a sleep." Quickly, Pat injected the initial dose of relaxant, rendering the young man unconscious. Then, with a steady hand - the second - paralysing the muscles in preparation for accustomed intubation. With nothing further to do with his hands, Pat squeezed until his nails dug into the palms and they bled.

For there was to be no intubation and with no air entry, Simon's heart slowly wound down and was still, his body held in Don's arms to the end.

****

Once again, Pat stared out of the open cottage window. It was evening and there was an April chill in the air. He closed it and continued to look across the valley, misty frost, swirling to carpet the fields. In the distance, dusk was beginning to fall over the hills.

Bless me Father, for I have sinned. It is twelve years since my last confession.

What is the nature of your sin, my son?

Father, today I killed a man.

Murder is indeed a serious crime, my son.

'Twas a mercy killing Father. All in the fecking line of duty.

Ah...Duty is an equally serious business. Sometimes duty must supersede the pull of the conscience. Go in peace, my son.

"*Why am I justifying this?* Pat said aloud to his reflection. Though he knew he would probably continue to ask the question for years to come.

Would you have let an animal suffer in that way, my son?

But, he was not an animal, Father. He was a warm, intelligent, thinking human being, soon to have a son.

So, what was the alternative? To let him die slowly, painfully, his body broken beyond repair? Would that have appeased your conscience?

No, no...no!

Denying him water perhaps, so not to prolong the agony?

No, Father...no.

And what of his family? Your pain pales when you consider their agony. Now, was there really an alternative?

Pat reached for the Bushmills and, sipping silently focused on the dignity of the situation. Then, he turned and took his sleeping wife in his arms and held her close.

Patrick Sean Michael O'Cleary III was born with the first watery rays of the sun at dawn. He was handed pink and puckered to his father who wept at the miracle of life once again.

And, two weeks later, to the day, another child was born. This time to Juliet, with her family gathered around her protectively: A son, Ethan...named by his dead father. He was a fine healthy boy who would thrive and grow in the sweet, fresh air of the Yorkshire hills and dales.

One day, before too long, the child and his mother would be visited by a man bringing flowers: A man fulfilling a promise, so, that when he was old enough to understand, the boy could be told that his father's last thought was of him and his mother.

And that he was loved more than life itself.

At Arbor Low (Ancient Monument)
By
Jane Croft

How well the ancients understood
Divine geometry; how well
They understood its sacred force,
Its synergy with earth and stone,
The rhythms of the running year,
And cycles of the sun and moon.

How well they understood the depth
Of human need for things sublime
Transcending mere mortality;
The power of awe to strengthen faith
And speak of esoteric planes,
And mysteries of death and birth.

How well the ancients understood
The power of place to summon thought:
This bank, and ditch, and ring of stones,
This grassy mound where old gods sleep,
Awake a primal need in us
And tease with secrets aeons deep.

Food For Thought
By
Mary Belfield

Annie had been trained as a Cook whilst working in London for Lord Stanley Stafford and his wife Lady Eleanor. She had initially been employed as a Lady's Maid but when Mrs Banks, the Cook, neared retirement she had been told that she would become her replacement. There was tittle tattle amongst the staff that their Esteemed Employees were 'feeling the pinch', as Mrs Banks had described it.

"I reckons they can't afford to 'ire a proper Cook like me so's they'se making do with thee Annie," she said. " Lady Eleanor wants me to learn you but I reckons it's an impossible job!" she continued.

Annie just bit back the furious retort and thought," *Cheeky sod. That old battleaxe never even went to school but thinks she's better that everyone else."* Annie's Mother had wanted something better than domestic work for her youngest and had insisted that she went to school. The family were very proud that their Annie was ,"working as a lady's maid away down in London."

"Oh I'm sure I'll do alright under your expert tuition," she said giving the older woman a sickly sweet smile. She removed her frilly, muslin cap from her beautiful head of brown curls and, gritting her teeth, tugged on a large, plain, buckram headpiece to drown her crowning glory. Rolling up her sleeves Annie tried not to cringe as she pulled on the elasticated arm coverings. They looked just like the legs of Mrs Banks' bloomers that were drying in the washhouse.

"Right lass let's get started. You're doing a proper job now not prancing around titivating her Ladyship... or yourself," added the Cook wagging her finger and staring at the girl. "You look a bit 'ot. Open that window and let in some fresh air. It'll p'raps blow away that 'orrible smell you keeps on waftin around."

Annie's red countenance was nothing to do with the temperature, and the horrible smell was the 'Evening In Paris' perfume given to her by Jack the Stableman. She forced her feet to move over to the wooden bench where her obnoxious tutor was waiting to instil some culinary knowledge to the unwilling and hostile pupil.

For the next few weeks she suffered non-accidental skin burns, chapped hands and cuts on every finger. But, worst of all, were the sarcastic, demeaning humiliating comments that she suffered at the hands of her instructress. Every night she would lie next to Jack in his loft above the stables telling him that she was going to leave and try to find a position elsewhere. Jack who was captivated by the beautiful young girl and was terrified of losing her kept trying to re-assure her. "The old witch will be leaving soon, Annie and you won't ever have to see her again."

"But that's not enough, Jack. She will be moving into that little cottage at the far end of the estate that the Staffords have given her. She will have peace, tranquillity and a good endowment and will live the life of Riley while we will be stuck here. She doesn't deserve it, Jack," said Annie her voice rising whilst her closed fists repeatedly thumped the mattress.

Jack thought hard and long about his dilemma . Each night Annie became more and more angry about her treatment by the tyrannical cook and her all-consuming desire for retribution. Finally, the young man disclosed to his lover the outlandish plan that had been forming in his mind for some time. He wondered if Annie would shun his scheme but she was ecstatic and insisted that they should begin their preparations immediately.

Some weeks later Mrs Banks retired from her post at Halcyon House and was driven by the stableman to her new abode, deep in the forest on the Halcyon Estate. Jack helped her with the unpacking and settling in to her new home. Just before he left he carried in a large pot full of a deliciously smelling stew and a bottle of her favourite elderberry wine.

"These are extra presents from Annie for helping her to become your replacement," he said. The elderly lady smiled at the broad-shouldered young man and said, "Thank 'er very much but just remind 'er that she still has a long way to go before she can fully replace me."

The young man just smiled. When Jack returned the following day to retrieve the stew pot and bury her body he installed his lover in the cottage eulogizing, "It didn't take quite as long as you thought it would Mrs Banks."

Slopsin
By
Graham Godfrey

Mishamoto, camp commandant, commander of life and death. Why didn't I bow down to him? Kow-tow to him? Why did I smile defiantly?

I knew I'd feel the impact of his baton. Smell and taste the iron of my blood slowly oozing from the sockets of my spat out teeth; from torn lips smashed to a pulp like raw liver.

Yet I kept doing it. Anything to get back to my tiny dream room. Four feet by four feet by four feet of bamboo cane walls, open to the beating rain or the searing sun flushing out my sweat. Always wet. Cramped, squatting in my own faeces and pee. Another five days in solitary. Wonderful. Away from the smell and daily horrors of my decaying and dying comrades. That smell of gangrenous rotting flesh grabs the back of my throat, clawing at it until I retch uncontrollably.

Yes, I want to be in here. The rat rice soup once a day. The pain of the beatings and cramp racking through my body, gradually building until the endorphins of my brain kick in. I am the camp doctor. Heal thyself. No way! *This* is what I want. Away from watching my so-called patients live their death day by day.

The beating every morning, now always in my balls, seems to accelerate and concentrate the morphemic centre of my brain.

Mishamato enjoyed it this morning. His connection was better

126

than a Stanley Mathews goal. Here it comes! That rush in my head, a buzz of ecstatic pain.

Yes I'm drifting... The bamboo walls of my cage become the bamboo wallpaper of Mrs. Maud's guesthouse in Blackpool.

She was *all* landlady. Ruby red lips, huge boobs, and bum trying to burst out of her gaudy red, green and yellow floral dress; worn over those wrinkled blue stockings. Always the same morning greetings:

"Enjoying yourselves, my loves?"

"Eggs are fresh!"

"Extra slice o' bacon this morning!"

"Bit windy. But rain overnight means you'll not get sand in you chips or stuck to your candy floss."

"Don't forget your towels and buckets and spades!"

Real treat today. Dad says we can go to the Pleasure Beach. Even have two rides! But which? What do I want?

Yeah, Big Dipper and Sky Rockets. High rides because it's like flying. Like leaving my body.

We go for the Sky Rockets first. Don't feel so good. Going round and round.

It made me feel dizzy, sicky, that did.

I was all right on the Big Dipper until the last drop. Mrs. Maud's breakfast was all down my new holiday shirt. Dad didn't half clout me one.

I'd give anything now for one of his clouts now. Really loved my old Dad.

Funny. Why am I crying in this cage? No! My room of bamboo.

Slops in. Slops out.

They are letting me push it out now, between the bars.

Takashi, the guard, a real family man, turns a blind eye and scuffs my faeces into the parched dry earth with his scruffy old boot.

It's my piss that gets to me. In the blazing sun it dries, giving off an acrid stench of ammonia-soaked, burnt toast.

Slopsin

Hey, this is great. The pain from my bloated bladder and blackened balls is kicking in the endorphins. The buzz is coming back. Recalling again.

Arny Eyre. Tall, lanky, like a long streak of piss. That's him, that smell.

Always peeing his trousers in the winter. Couldn't hold it on the walk to school through the snow and cold.

Miss Peacher would make him hang his wet short trousers on the radiator.

That same stink.

Still, it killed off the rotten egg smell of the Brussels sprouts being murdered by hours of boiling in the school kitchen.

Dorothy hated those Brussels sprouts as much as I did.

What was it she said?

"Come into my Dad's hen house and I'll show you where *my* eggs come from. You have to put your poker in first, then I can lay some of them."

That first time is now triggering many others.

Count them.

1 Dorothy.

2 Anne.

I keep losing count.

They keep dragging me out and bashing me.

Which number and name did I get to?

Damn. Have to start again.

Getting bored with going over the same ones.

Must remember the last.

What's her name?

I'm married to her.

Help me!

This morning's different. Beaten even harder. Four of them this time. Sounds of snapping bones. Just for pushing my faeces out.

Graham Godfrey

It's raining softly.
I'm feeling really slow.
I think I can see a rainbow through my bamboo walls.
I feel detached from my torn bloodied body.
Looking down on myself in my little barred cage.
Yet, in there, is a beautiful padded silk bed enclosed in oak sides.
So soft and long, I can lie fully out in it.
I climb in, stretch out, and drift into a dark sleep.
Wish I could take you all with me my dear friends.
Forgive me.
I leave the dream room of my memories for you.

129

Ladybower
By
Jane Croft

At Ladybower the past lives on:
The land retains an echo there,
A resonance of times long gone,
At Ladybower the past lives on.
Events impressed on earth and stone
Rebound upon the listening air.
At Ladybower the past lives on
The land retains an echo there.

The Lancasters fly swift and low
Along the mirror of the lake,
Their moonlit shapes no shadows throw,
The Lancasters fly swift and low.
The cockpit glass no pilots show,
No sound their great propellers make.
The Lancasters fly swift and low
Along the mirror of the lake.

At Ladybower the shades remain
Where past and present coincide
And olden forms appear again,
At Ladybower the shades remain
And wood and hill and crag contain
The place where different worlds collide;
At Ladybower the shades remain
Where past and present coincide.

*Author note: Ladybower Reservoir, in the heart of the Dark Peak,
is irrevocably associated with 617 Squadron and its Lancaster*

bombers. They practised here for the 'bouncing bomb' raids on the German dams in WW2. The place is powerfully atmospheric and the legends about it are many, among them the one I have used as the inspiration for this poem.

Lost Lad - A Tale of the Dark Peak
By
Jane Croft

His duty took him to the hills that day,
And love perhaps; for with his father gone
Who else should mind his mother and the farm?
He saw the massing cloud on Derwent Edge
And Whinstone Lee, and knew the snow would come
Before the day was done, and he must go
And fetch the flock down safe into the fold.
He told his mother he'd be back ere long;
Then, whistling to his faithful dog, set out.
They'd barely reached Back Tor before the snow
Began: mere flecks at first, insidious,
Beguiling thought with hope of time enough.
Undaunted yet, the boy pursued his task
And sought the sheep across the open slope.

With no more warning then the blizzard struck.
In minutes it reduced the view to feet
Until the world was shrunk to flying flakes
That clotted as they fell and palled the earth,
Enshrouding rock and turf and heath with ice.
Bewildered by the storm they stumbled on
The boy and dog, both cringing from the cold,
Heads down against the biting wind, half blind,
Direction swallowed in confusion's midst.
All thought of sheep forgotten now they found

Lost Lad

A jutting rock and huddled in the lee
Together for companionship and warmth.

For hours and hours they kept the hope alive
Of coming home again, or being found
At least, until the hope grew cold and faint,
And, finally, the boy reached out a hand
And fumbled for a stone to scratch the words
Upon the rock – a testament of faith –
And, having written, closed his eyes and drowsed.
And for a while the dog kept vigil there,
Until he too succumbed, and fell asleep.

For days the neighbours searched but found no trace
Of them; for days the anxious mother watched
And hoped and prayed no doubt, but all in vain.
It was a shepherd, in the spring, who found
The pair, and read upon the rock the words
LOST LAD. He built a cairn to mark the spot
That he might recognise the place again
Before descending to impart the news;
And so the boy and dog came home at last.

In after years their monument has grown
For many here have paused to place a stone
Upon the cairn, and to reflect awhile
And, by remembering, keep faith with them.

*Author note: This poem is based on a well-known local story.
About a century ago, 13 year old Abraham Lowe and his dog
were caught in a blizzard while attempting to bring a flock down
off the hills behind Ladybower. Both perished. A large cairn- Lost
Lad - marks the place where they were eventually found.*

Lost For Words
By
Jean Mallender

Autumn leaves blew across the lane as the mini-bus drew up beside the stone cottage. It was surrounded by rubble. The building had been totally refurbished, rising from the devastation like a pustule - harsh and yellow, without the softening cover of lichens.

The driver hit his horn, then jumped down and went round to open the passenger door.

'Come on Emily, you'll be OK,' said the blonde haired woman, hustling her small daughter in front of her down the rubbish-strewn path. The child clung to a teddy. Her eyes were half closed and her jaw clenched as her mother swung her up onto the bus.

'You'll see she goes into the nursery, won't you?' she said.

The driver shut the door as he replied, 'Aye, she'll be fine when the other kids get on.' The woman turned, pulling her silk housecoat round her and marching back inside without a second glance.

The bus went the hundred yards to the next cottage, a twin to the other - this being the 'before' version to the other's 'after'.

The driver turned round in the lane, wound down the window and shouted, 'Ada! Ada!'

Through the arch of brambles over the gateway he could see a bent figure in a cap, digging in the vegetable plot.

'Morning,' said the man, then resumed digging as a small chubby woman with a halo of white curls bustled down the path.

'I'm not going,' said Ada. 'I'm too busy pickling. Thanks anyway. Oh, who's that you have in there?' Ada and the driver peered at the small child scrunched in the corner, quietly crying to herself. Ada's ruddy face folded into a smile.

'Have you shown Teddy my pussycats? Look, they are on the wall.' The child's eyes flicked to the window as she fixed on the two tabbies. 'You must have moved in next door. What's your name then?'

The driver shook his head. 'Doesn't speak, so her Mam said. Shame!' Ada pulled a red apple from her apron pocket.

'Here – for Teddy.' The child didn't stir as the driver placed the apple beside her.

'Bye Ada,' he called, and set off back down the lane.

In the modernised cottage, Diana was up the spiral stairs showering when the phone rang. She ignored it. Half an hour later, it rang again.

'Yes?' By now she was working on her laptop. 'Oh! Sorry…I *was* worried about her. She's OK then? Well, I expected she'd cry - she'll settle.' She paused to listen, then picked up a pen. 'I'll take the school's number again, though I think I have it.'

A knock on the door was an excuse to hang up. She smoothed her hair before opening it.

'Morning, I'm Ada. We live next door - me and my brother, John.' She thrust a gleaming jar of pickled beetroot at Diana. The jar had the same ruddy glow as Ada's face. She gave a gap-toothed smile, her arms resting on her lumpy bosom as she waited for a reaction to her gift.

'Thanks - I'm Diana - Di. Very kind.'

'Saw your little one this morning. Ah, crying she was.' Ada's green wellingtons were shedding crumbs of dried mud on Diana's pale floor. She stepped inside uninvited, and looked round.

'My, it's changed. Where've the walls gone?'

'I've refurbished - brought it into the twenty-first century. Gutted …New broom and all that,' said Di. Ada's eyes lit up - she knew about brooms. She stared at the hessian hangings on the wall.

'Anyway, it'll be nice when those sacks are down and you get some furniture,' she said. 'You could borrow my table…'

'No thanks, I have a table - there.' Di pointed to a low oblong platform, surrounded by squashy cushions. Ada nodded as she glanced about.

'If you don't mind my asking, where's your fire? It can get cold…'

'Blown air heating,' Di said, taking a deep breath. 'Very kind of you to bring these Miss…Ada.' Ada beamed.

'Come for a cup of tea this afternoon then,' Ada said. 'Anytime suits us.'

'Right, yah, thank-you.' Ada turned, her boots squeaking on the floor and shedding rings of mud.

Di pulled out her mobile as she shut the door and dialled. She launched into a description of her new neighbour.

'Mrs. Noah, that's her. She lives with her brother. Weird!' She paused. 'Mm? Emily's OK. Cried this morning. The good thing is she'll not be a chatterbox.' Di held the phone away from her ear, as the person on the other end of the line erupted. 'Steady on, I meant that she'd be no trouble. It's six months since she spoke.' She looked at her watch before hanging up and starting work again.

Ada and John were welcoming, as Di and her dark-haired daughter stepped into their porch that afternoon. Three basket chairs were crammed against the wall. John motioned for Di to sit, but before she could, he swept off his cap and wafted the cushions with it, releasing a cloud of cat hairs.

'Ada's not cleaned today,' he said. Di gathered her black linen skirt round her, before lowering herself onto the seat.

Ada was back with a tea tray. She poured the tea from a silver teapot into china cups, handed them round and sat down herself. There was milk for the girl.

'Now, this is nice,' she said, patting the child. 'And what is she called then - wouldn't tell me this morning?'

'Emily,' said Di.

'Emily?' John asked. 'We call one of our cats Emily.' He turned to the child. 'Would you liked to see her?'

Di intervened. 'She'll not want to...' But Emily followed John round the back of the cottage, half-smiling.

'Dad works away, does he?' asked Ada.

'Divorced,' said Di. 'I left London to make a fresh start.'

'Must be hard with a child.'

'Yes - but Dave insisted a child should stay with its mother. We had a nanny before.'

'Has Emily always been dumb?'

'Oh no, it was after...' Di shuffled.

'Misses daddy does she?' Ada nodded.

'We manage,' said Di. 'I'm my own boss. I can work anywhere. All I need is a laptop and a mobile.'

'Ah.' Ada's eyes had glazed over, then suddenly focussed on the back of her hand. She slapped it hard. 'Got you. Cats and fleas go together - fact of life,' she said. The porch roof began to rattle. Ada looked up. 'Going to be gales tonight.'

Emily came running back smiling. She pulled at her mother's hand, her mouth opening and closing.

'Yes darling I know,' said Di, 'but we have to go now.'

'She wants you to look at the kittens,' Ada told her.

'Some other time.' Emily's face closed up again and she stood with her arms by her side as Di rose.

'Thank-you for the tea,' Di murmured, then took her silent daughter back home through the gathering storm.

Di didn't sleep well that night as the wind and rain howled round the house. She rose early, to make a good start on e-mails while Emily was asleep. She switched on the kettle, before putting some bread in the toaster. Then she moved to her laptop.

'Damn.' The screen was dead. She'd left it on all night so

she'd have to plug in and charge it up. She decided to have a coffee first, but the kettle was stone cold. She flicked a light switch - no light. Then she realised there was no power. She grimaced - no drink, no toast and no laptop.

The phone call to the electricity board only got an automated service.

'We are aware of the problem in your area. We hope to have the power restored by...' The voice tailed off followed by a series of clicks. Di stamped her feet. All she could think of were her deadlines- with only a phone to communicate she was lost.

Today was Saturday. She would have to drive up to London - she could just about make it, but what about Emily? She couldn't take her... Then she had an idea... Dare she ask them - it was only for a few hours?

'Emily,' she called. 'Emily, get up - mummy has to go to London.'

At 8.15 Di was hammering on Ada and John's cottage door with Emily and Teddy by her side.

Di was all smiles and explanations - power-cut - work - London - ending with, 'Could you possibly look after Emily for me?'

Ada smiled. 'Course - it'll be a treat.' She enveloped Emily in her arms. 'Let's see, one of my chuck-a-loos has laid an egg especially for you. Shall we fetch it?' Emily's body relaxed and she nodded as Ada waved her mother away.

It was evening when Di returned.

'Come in,' said Ada, 'Emily's fine - follow me.'

Di pushed her way sideways through the crowded passage, past the cupboards that filled it, into the small back room. A fire blazed in the black-leaded range and an oil lamp glowed on a hefty sideboard. It illuminated a large table, covered in a peacock-patterned cloth. Sepia photos hung on the walls. John, his cap still on, sat reading a newspaper.

'Oh dear,' said Di, 'still no power? Mine's on.'

John laughed. 'What power?' he said. 'We've never bothered

wi' electric.'

'Nah,' said Ada, 'I likes the nice soft light from a lamp.'

'What about washing, ironing, TV?'

'There's the wireless,' said Ada, 'always got batteries.'

Di sniffed. What was that acrid smell? What had she done leaving Emily with these two simpletons from the Stone Age?

'I'd better take Emily home now please.'

'She's there,' said Ada pointing.

Di's eyes, now used to the gloom, noticed that the table, underneath the cloth, was enclosed in chicken wire. She bent to look.

'What have you got here - *hens*?' Emily peeped out at her. She was crouched down holding something. It was a tiny chicken.

'Yes,' said John, 'brought them in from the storm.'

Di recoiled. 'In the *house*?' She winced, but a sound made her stop. Emily had stepped forward, stroking the chicken.

'Ch...k.' Emily was trying to speak. 'Chuck, chuck-a-loo, chuck-a-loo, chuck-a-loo,' she said getting faster on each repetition. Then, 'Look M...Mummy.'

Ada and John began clapping and laughing. Ada hugged Emily, and John patted her as she said the words again and again.

In the midst of the noise and happiness Di stood quite still, and totally silent.

Emily held up the chick. Di put her hands behind her backing away. Ada's bright eyes took in the situation.

'Why don't you put the chick back with his mum, Emily?' she said, standing between the child and her mother.

Di took another step back: 'I...I...It's the feathers and the pointy beaks - pecking, pecking...' Her hands went up to her pale face.

Ada concentrated on Emily: 'You can always come back tomorrow. Can you think of any names for the chicks?'

'Chicks,' said Emily again. 'Name. Name - Mummy - Di - Dave - Dave - *Daddy*.' The last word was much louder. Emily was bent stroking a chick and letting the new experience of speaking tumble the words out of her mouth.

'Daddy, where's Daddy? Where's Daddy gone?' The horror

of what she was saying struck her. She clawed her way past Ada and buried her face in her mother's skirt sobbing.

Di's face crumpled and her breathing quickened. Their distress cut into the calm of the softly lit room. The hens began to cluck in alarm.

John stood up to put a steadying arm round Di's shoulder, his matted cardigan sleeve shedding hairs on Di's crisp navy jacket.

He spoke to his sister: 'Ada, get out the Christmas brandy.' Di allowed herself to be lowered into the old leather armchair, pulling the still-sobbing Emily onto her knee where she rocked her.

Di's eyes flicked a thank-you to Ada as she passed her a tot of brandy, which she downed in one gulp. She sighed heavily, squeezing her daughter.

'You are a clever girl, Emily,' Di said.

Ada bent towards them. 'She's helped me all day - haven't you?' Emily raised a tear-stained face.

'Was it eight eggs we collected?' Ada continued. She waited as Emily's head gave a shake.

'T...t...ten. It was ten,' she said, her chest still heaving.

'Ah yes, you're right. We used three for breakfast, and one for the scones. You made some scones didn't you?' She pronounced scones with a long 'o'.

Di took Ada's cue. 'Scones,' she asked, 'real scones?'

Emily pushed herself off her mother's knee and went out of the room. Ada nodded encouragingly at Di as Emily came back in carrying a plate of scones.

'For you M-mummy.' Di turned to Ada.

'Yes, she did them all by herself,' Ada said.

'Thank you. We'll take them home now.' She plucked at Emily's dark hair.

'I'll get the storm lantern and walk you down the lane,' said John.

'It's OK, I brought the car...' She paused, aware of the couple's amazement. 'It was out already,' she added. They wouldn't have a car and would walk everywhere of course, especially a mere hundred yards.

She felt the buzz of her mobile in her jacket pocket. 'Excuse me,' she said flicking the top open as she pulled it out. 'Yes? Sorry - can I ring you back? OK.' She turned to Ada and John. 'Really sorry about that.'

'Oh no,' Ada grinned, 'we enjoyed it. We've never been that close to a portable telephone.'

'Seen them in the village,' added John. 'Some of the youngsters look as if they're glued to their ears.' The old couple chortled at his joke.

'Ah!' Di was the one amazed now. Of course they wouldn't even have a telephone, never mind a mobile.

Ada turned to Emily. 'You can bring the plate back when you've eaten the scones.'

Emily nodded, calm once more. She glanced at the chickens, then whispered, 'Bye, bye,' as she followed her mother out.

Di shouted once more up the stairs: 'Night-night, Darling. Sleep tight.' She grabbed her mobile, then flopped down on one of the giant cushions.

She rang her mother. 'Sorry I couldn't chat when you rang, I'm home now...yes, we're fine.' She listened, eyes closed. 'As a matter of fact, Emily actually spoke today. How? It's a long story...What did she say? Chick. She said chick.'

Di explained how she'd been forced into using her neighbours as baby-sitters. She shrugged at her mother's disapproval. 'Look, I'm awfully tired, can we chat tomorrow? Yes, I know it's important.' She stood up and paced round as she listened. 'Right, look, I'll ring you in the morning. Bye.'

She stood, smoothing her hair. *Yes mother,* she thought, *they are ancient and live in the past, but Emily spoke...For them, not me. Although...*

Out loud she shouted, 'Dave, you are a *bastard*, leaving me with Emily...' She covered her hands with her eyes when she realised what she had said. 'Damn him. Damn everything!' She flung her mobile onto a cushion and went up to bed.

The Sparks Fly Upward
By
Phil Foster

'Yet man is born unto trouble, as the sparks fly upward.'
Eliphaz, the Temanite, *Job* 5:7

'Burn!' shouted the crowd. 'Burn to a cinder!'

Jack Catesby looked up. Shading his eyes with a hand, he tried to focus on that one constant yet flickering speck of light in the night sky. It should not have been blinking, of course, for it was not a star – and the atmosphere was not *that* thick. But his view was partially obscured through the gathering wisps of smoke as the flames began to take hold.

As tears came to his eyes, Jack pulled out a handkerchief and gave an unconvincing cough. Then, feeling a tap on his shoulder, he jumped.

'You should retreat, Councillor,' the loud voice said. Jack turned. 'I cannot share in your history, granted,' it continued, 'but I do *know* something of it. May I suggest that someone with my name and rank ought to be allowed the greater proximity?' The man chuckled and a few others joined in.

'Of course, Mr. President.' Jack adjusted his gaze and slowly moved back to join the others. Guy La Guerre turned and walked over to a nearby platform. After mounting it he gave a nod of satisfaction as he looked round at the smiling, twisted faces.

Jack scanned the heavens, fascinated. The wood began to crackle, spitting out cousins to that Great Light. Spectacular they may have been, but they were far more ephemeral. Like mayflies dancing on a pond, they lived out their brief yet glorious lives. *But who could say that* we *may not be just like them? It's all relative...* He gave a sigh to accompany his thoughts.

La Guerre addressed the crowd. 'I do not intend to say much, *mes chers amis*; we all know why we are here. We are gathered this evening to remember...'

To destroy, thought Jack.

'... our mistakes.'

But not *to learn*, the thoughts continued.

'As someone once said: "He who does not learn the lessons of history is destined to repeat the errors."' La Guerre pointed upward and took a deep breath. 'Thus, we have inaugurated this special Memorial Evening.'

At the going down of the sun and in the morning... Jack resisted the temptation to tap his feet. He wondered whether he should sneak a look at his atomic timepiece with the infra-red illumination and multi-digit readout. Instead, he pulled out an old pocket watch and chain. Turning it slightly towards the flames, he ran a finger over the dial: the small hand pointed to eleven. *One minute past midnight*, he thought.

'I have spoken long enough,' La Guerre turned ninety degrees to his right and stretched out an arm to indicate the pyre burning behind him. 'These flames are far more eloquent than I could ever be.'

You can say that again! Jack allowed himself half a smile at the irony behind his thought.

'There is, however, one other person I would like you to hear before you bring forward your ...'

'Offerings?' someone shouted out.

Sacrifices, Jack thought, on the altar of expediency.

La Guerre nodded. '*Merci, mon brave*. Most helpful. That was *exactly* the word for which I was searching.' He turned and smiled at a tall, blond-haired man who was standing to his right. 'I call upon you all now to welcome Chuck Armstrong, our new Vice-President.'

As La Guerre initiated the crowd into a thunderous round of applause, three scantily-clad young women began to wave items of underwear in Armstrong's direction. They were supported by more than one piercing whistle.

Never before has a title been more appropriate, Jack thought. He clapped slowly and mechanically as La Guerre's assistant stepped to the front.

'Welcome! Welcome everyone.' Armstrong clasped his hands together and held them above his head. Then he began to shake them in a time-honoured gesture of victory. A broad grin stretched across his square-jawed face as the gathering began to cheer. 'And thank *you* Mr. President...or may I call you "Guy"?' La Guerre smiled back and began to unbutton his tie. 'This will, I hope, be the first of many...'

Oh no! God help us.

'...Memorial Evenings which we will celebrate together.'

Jack began to shiver as the fire really started to take hold.

'Thank you, thank you all,' The American said. The clapping became rhythmic in order to accompany the chant: 'Armstrong! Armstrong! Armstrong!' But the crowd hushed as he stretched out his arms to the front and moved them up and down, palms aimed at the ground. A gust of wind fanned the flames.

'Friends, you know me...'

I certainly do, Jack thought.

Armstrong placed a hand on his chest. 'I hold now – and always have held – your best interests at heart "'

Cant; rhetoric; mindless platitudes. A blind man could see it.

'And so I thought I might share with you – slightly paraphrased, of course – a few thoughts inspired by one of my illustrious ex-countrymen, Abraham Lincoln, a.k.a. "Honest Abe" .'

You're as honest as the day is short.

'But first, let me say this: You all have a stake in our

community ...'

I know where I'd like to put mine...

'And many of you come from cultures which have, in times past, enjoyed celebrating with bonfires.' He turned slightly, held out a hand towards the flames, and continued: 'Of course, bonfires have had a long history; they've been dated to pagan times.'

Sounds like one of your new girlfriends. Jack felt like snapping his fingers. *So that's why you like them...*

'It's a similar case with fireworks. They go back almost as far.'

If only you could.

'Take Chin Ho for example.'

Please – take him!

A thick-joweled Chinese near the front slowly bent forward. He hid his reddening face as Armstrong continued: 'As I'm sure you're all aware Chin's ancestors actually *invented* fireworks.'

Jack gave Chin a cold stare.

'And since our oriental friend is the most prominent citizen of Chinese extraction, it seemed only fitting to invite him to organize tonight's display.'

'Chin! Chin! Chin!' went the cry.

I'd have used his other name, Jack thought.

Armstrong put up a hand. As the chanting died down he turned back, looked at Jack and nodded. 'Then we have Councillor Catesby here: for some strange reason, November the 5th seems to mean something to the English.' He winked at La Guerre. 'Now I'm not entirely sure as to *why* I feel so uneasy, Mr. President, but I've just spotted Jack rubbing his hands. If I were you I wouldn't stand too close to the fire with him close by ...'

The mob erupted into uncontrolled laughter. 'Please!' Armstrong shouted. 'I've only just started. In honour of our leader, I'd like to say something about *la belle France.*'

The Vice-President put on an exaggerated Gallic accent. 'Guy: our citizens have a reputation for enjoying the odd firework ...although some of us have been inclined to go a bit too far.' He made a slashing motion across his throat. 'I am all in favour of

144

enjoying ourselves; only…let us ensure that we do not lose our heads!'

More laughter. Someone began to hum *La Marseillaise.*

La Guerre rose to his feet and gave a mock-salute. 'I trust, Chuck, that you have something to say about your *own* people …'

Armstrong grinned. 'But of course,' he said, puffing out his chest, 'I've always been true-blue.'

Can't disagree with that. Jack thought, looking at the three highly-exposed young women again. As they were eying up their hero and whispering in one another's ears, one of then stepped back open-mouthed from the others. Her companions laughed.

'I have much in common with you, Mr. President,' Armstrong continued. 'July 4th, 1776 and July 14^{th,} 1789: Independence Day; Bastille Day... not much time separates our former great national celebrations.'

'And our late-lamented homelands used to be friends,' La Guerre interjected.

'True enough, Guy, true enough.' Armstrong took a breath, raised his voice theatrically, and pointed a finger in the air: 'In February 1778, eleven years before the French Revolution, the Treaty of Alliance between France and the United States was signed. And *why* was this?' He paused before answering his own rhetorical question. 'Remember the Marquis de Lafayette? He was recruited for the Continental Army by U. S. agents in Paris and became one of its greatest generals.' The new Vice-President coughed. Someone brought forward a glass of water. He took a sip, conveyed his thanks, and resumed. 'So when, in October 1777, General Burgoyne was defeated at the Battle of Saratoga, France was impressed.'

Many in the crowd were looking at each other. Their faces held puzzled expressions.

Jack's eyes were squinted. *A history lesson? This is a change of tack. Where are you going with this, Armstrong?*

The American rubbed the back of his neck and cleared his throat. 'Excuse me,' he said, pausing to take another sip. 'Many years later, the Statue of Liberty was gifted by the French people to welcome the "poor and huddled masses" to the shores of The New

World. And so my friends, I want to ask you this: Are *we* not "poor"? Are *we* not "huddled"? Are *we* not "the masses"?'

You'd better watch him, Guy: he's pitching for President!

There was a buzz now about the crowd: many people nodded; some whispered to each other. 'An icon to *both* nations,' he continued, jabbing both index fingers in the air simultaneously. 'How was it then that "Liberty" could not save either country in the end? For when the ultimate test came, she fell …' The breeze picked up, appearing to add strength to Armstrong's point. Then it became still, as if awaiting an answer.

The crowd was totally quiet now; hanging on every word.

Jack ruffled his hair back, digging into his scalp as the thought came: *Oh, Lord, they're lapping it up. Save us from the educated populist!*

'Because the alliance was not wide enough?' La Guerre suggested.

'Spot on, Mr. President! You are so astute.'

Crawler, sycophant! It's no wonder you got where you are.

'However,' La Guerre's assistant spread his arms out wide, 'the future is now in our hands.'

One digit per minute, Jack thought.

'Today, my friends, we do not need generals. Oh, they may have had their uses centuries ago,' said the American, gazing upwards, 'but our night sky gives testimony as to where that sort of militaristic thinking can lead.'

Armstrong held up a hand to quell the gathering ripple of applause. *Clever*, thought Jack, catching himself in order not to join in. *The old orator's trick: say something everyone can agree with, then, in order to appear modest, stop the crowd from showing too much enthusiasm.*

Armstrong's eyes fixed on the gathering once more. 'No; let us rather look outward – to each other – for our present gathering is a truly international one. '

You're behind the times, Chuck.

'What we need is a *new* revolution. One which encompasses us all: American, British, Chinese, French, Russian…Which reminds me, friends – I've been remiss. I haven't mentioned our esteemed brother, Councillor Mikhail Pavel Brönstein yet.'

A stern, dark-haired man gazed on. '*Tavarich*: it is thanks in part to your ancestors that we are here today; that we have a second chance if you like. I wish I had a crate of vodka to help us celebrate. Take a bow, Mikhail.' Armstrong's nod was slight. Almost immediately, someone slapped the Russian in the back, making his cap fall off. He cursed and bent to retrieve it; for a second time the crowd laughed uproariously.

And now you're sprinkling in a bit of humour again. Jack nodded reluctantly. *You're a real pro, Armstrong, I'll give you that.*

'But seriously, folks, I am humbled by the thought of the offerings which I know you are all so impatient to give. Which brings me finally to Lincoln: Tonight, if you will, we have a *new* nation. Brought forth from the ruins of its predecessors, it stands out like a beacon, just like Honest Abe.'

You couldn't hold a Roman candle to him.

'As the Great Backwoodsman might have said: "It is altogether fitting and proper that we should do this … because you are about to give up your last full measure of devotion".'

Jack had a crazy vision of a skeletal Lincoln, beard hanging from the skull, taking off his top hat, standing on his head, and spinning around in a frock coat on a tomb in the style of an old-time break-dancer.

'I have very little more to say, my friends, except...' the American walked over to his right. Standing at the edge of the platform, he raised an arm, causing the crowd to bisect on cue. 'As we are about to bring forward our offerings let us remember how much we all have in common.'

Not as much as you might think...

Two figures walked through the gangway. A stuffed mannequin wearing a smart grey uniform was brought forward, carried on a stretcher. Decorated with four stars on each epaulette, its chest pocket was covered with multi-coloured ribbons; a braided cap sat upon its head. The stretcher-bearers laid their burden on the floor close to the fire, stood by and waited.

Next, two other people carried a similar dummy, this time dressed in brown. If the insignia on each shoulder was different (a crown, a pip, and crossed sword and baton), its brass hat was very familiar. It was taken, like the first, to the side of the fire and rested there. Soon after, a third mannequin, in a blue uniform with one thick ring and three narrower ones adorning both sleeves, was laid beside the other two.

All was quiet as Brönstein carried forward three crown-shaped laurel leaves. 'A fitting tribute to our honoured dead,' he said through pursed lips. 'Let us bestow on them a posthumous promotion before they are cremated.' The Russian placed the crowns on top of the dummies' heads and, giving them a mock-salute, declared: 'All-hail to our fallen heroes: a General of the Army; a Field Marshall; and an Admiral of the Fleet!'

Someone began a slow hand-clap. Gradually, everyone joined in; many also booed.

Armstrong sat down and La Guerre took his place. 'Now!' he cried, turning to the stretcher-bearers. The dummies were hoisted up and thrown into the flames to the accompaniment of raucous cheers. The Frenchman spoke to the crowd once more. 'As we celebrate our freedom, let us now bring forward our own prospective offerings. Anything can be considered, no matter how small.'

A woman waved a Bible. 'How about this?' she asked.

La Guerre nodded. 'It is perfect – perfect because it is full of outmoded and guilt-ridden dogma calculated to hold us back. Keeping it would be a crime. Burn it, *Madame*, burn it!'

Whoops of delight accompanied the woman as she ran forward and cast the book into the flames.

'Hey! Is this any use?' A man at the back hoisted up a telescope.

'Not any more,' La Guerre replied, 'Why look to the skies for help? We are settled now; the masters of our own destinies. So, please,' he stretched out an arm towards the flames, 'be my guest …'

'Burn! Burn! Burn!' shouted the mob as the offending instrument was dragged to its fate.

Someone held up another book. The Frenchman put a hand to shield his brow. 'I can't see the title,' he said, shaking his head.

The man shrugged, turned the book round, and read out slowly: '*Fundamental Principles of Interplanetary Travel* – says it was written by a Nobel Prize winner.' He whistled and tousled his hair. 'That's impressive, Mr. President; maybe we shouldn't –'

'Burn it!' La Guerre interrupted.

'But –'

'I said *burn* it!' The man bowed his head and trudged forward as La Guerre gave him an icy stare. His half-hearted throw into the flames was greeted by a change in the President's countenance.

'Science has its uses, of course; I would be the first person to admit it.' The Frenchman smiled. 'After all, without it, none of us would be here.' Some people nodded. 'But then again, look what science has *done,*' he continued, pointing to the brightness in the heavens. 'Without it, none of us would need to be here!'

'Down with science!' someone screamed. '*Vive* La Guerre!' shouted another.

The more things change… Jack thought, translating the well-known French saying.

'Why retain a book which no longer has any value?' La Guerre continued, wagging his finger at the Great Light. 'Does anyone wish to go there?'

'No!' went the cry.

'Could anyone live there?'

'No!' This time the shouts were louder.

'And what, by definition, is the last planet in the universe that could be terraformed?'

This time La Guerre did not wait for a reply. 'No,' he said, 'it could never be made fit for human habitation; not if we had a million years.'

A woman, one of Armstrong's three lightly-dressed friends, fished out a book from her bag; the naked bodies on the front cover left little to the imagination. 'You wouldn't want us to burn *this* would you, Mr. President?'

'Of course not!' La Guerre tilted his head and grinned. 'We

149

are here to celebrate life, are we not?'

A man at the front held up a large, hard-back book. 'This looks a bit dodgy, Mr. President. Shall I ...?' La Guerre read the title and author with no difficulty:

Mein Kampf
von
Adolph Hitler

'Not at all!' the Frenchman demurred, 'You must not believe everything that you've heard about him.' He clenched his hand into a fist. 'It means "My Struggle". Change "My" to "Our" and it sums-up our situation rather nicely, don't you think?'

'Well ...' the man flicked through some of the pages and began to scratch his head. 'I know a bit of German myself and some of the words do seem a bit warlike ...'

La Guerre waved the objection away. 'I'm sure that you've just taken him out of context. Please give it to me.' The President stretched down a hand.

Obediently, the man passed it over. 'You have closed the book,' the Frenchman said, looking at the man closely. 'Do not close your mind. Herr Hitler had many good ideas which may well be worth our consideration.' La Guerre jutted out his chest. Then he held the book aloft and shook it. 'Never forget this: in times of great crisis, difficult decisions must sometimes be made. What always counts is the greater good.'

Jack imagined ranks of men marching and singing: they were carrying flaming torches.

Many other people came forward, but Jack blocked out the details. He was in a bubble; pondering the new inverse relationship between an object's positive utility and the likelihood of its retention.

Finally, La Guerre made the announcement:

'And now, my friends, what we've all been waiting for. Chin: the fireworks. Let's party!'

The Chinese stepped onto the platform and turned to the crowd. Then he raised his hand slowly and dramatically let it fall.

The sky changed from black to red. *The two-legged sheep are happy*, Jack mused as he consulted his watch again, *zero hour and all's not well*. As the rockets went up, the engineer was reminded of his journey: the "return flight" which became a one-way ticket. It was meant to be a three-month stint. But then the news reports came about the *other* rockets...

And he thought of how it *must* have been:

The horror and shock on the faces of the infants as they buried their heads in their parents' chests when the witches flew over on plutonium broomsticks to the sound of the sirens amidst impotent screams in the mouths of the children as they realized the truth that the nightmare was real and everyone knew they could not be protected from the bogeyman poised to snatch all that was loved and burn it to a cinder in a gigantic furnace kindled by man to destroy the woman who gave him birth.

The heavens were illuminated by exploding colours as beautiful patterns were spewed out into the newly-breathable air. On and on the display went, until it culminated in a dizzying kaleidoscope and a shattering bang. The biggest rocket of all had exploded, eliciting gasps and highlighting jaws hungry for more. Spontaneous applause broke out; then, finally, there was silence. In the heavens, acrid smoke disfigured the face of one who had once been so beautiful. Jack pondered the implications: Hope for the future or omen of death?

Terraform or Terror Form?

He looked round amidst the stillness and thought of a canal. Liquid once flowed there and soon, thanks to human ingenuity, it would do so again.

Would it be water? Or would it be blood?

They had discussed it in Council.

As La Guerre stood to address the assembly, Jack felt the thudding in his chest as he anticipated the rehearsed challenge. When the moment came, would his courage fail him?

'*Mes Amis*: tonight we have witnessed a marvel to which we

have all contributed. Remember our new maxim? "Eat, drink and be merry, for tomorrow we die."' Many eyes were drawn up to that Great Light. 'Let us therefore dedicate ourselves to the pursuit of happiness.' He winked at Armstrong. 'But, since this is a democracy, I say to you all: if there are *any* here who would dispute our right to so-celebrate let them come forward and identify themselves, or else remain silent.' La Guerre gestured expansively with his right arm.

The crowd was silent as the fire burned weakly in the shadow of *Olympus Mons*. The long-extinct volcano bore witness to the vestiges of laurel leaves, now reduced to dust.

As tears filled his eyes, Jack thought he detected one spark, stubbornly refusing to be extinguished.

'Yes,' he said, slowly raising an arm, *'I* would.' Shakily, he walked toward the platform. La Guerre and Armstrong looked at each other grim-faced as he climbed the scaffold, turned, and began to speak.

'Citizens of Mars: do not be deceived ...'

From somewhere in the background, Jack heard the snap of a laser rifle ...

The Price of Freedom
By
Colyn Broom

Gavin stood perfectly still. A sharp breeze whistled around him blowing his hair, its shrill lonely howl echoing in his ears. He took in a long, deep breath of the cool, fresh air – holding it for a moment; allowing it to tingle inside his nostrils and bite at his lungs. He could see his breath momentarily as he exhaled before the air stream whisked it away – gone forever.

It was time, and he knew it – no point in prolonging the inevitable. He bent his head, looking beyond his feet and past the metal work. Down, down, down – finally focusing his gaze on the murky ice-cold waters of the fast-flowing river. He could see several boats and people moving around on them; they looked *so* tiny – *so* toy-like. If he reached out his hand, it seemed like he could pick them up.

Adrenalin coursed through his body and his knees shook – was it nerves, the cold or both? Gavin took another deep breath. *No regrets, no looking back. It's* your *time to be free of everything – to soar like a bird, to be an eagle, just for a few seconds before...*

He raised his arms from his sides into a crucifix position, the blood pumping in his ears as it raced through his veins and around his body. He leant slowly forward.

The wind whipped at his face sweeping his hair back tightly

153

against his head. He could hardly breathe as his jacket flapped and snapped with his increasing velocity. His entire body screamed with exhilaration; he was free. He closed his eyes and waited for the finalé ... then a huge shudder rippled through his entire body.

It wasn't quite what he'd expected. Gavin opened his right eye. Then slowly, his left. He was standing on a hard, flat surface. A chilly mist surrounded him – and there was pressure on both of his upper arms.

In front of him was a figure, a man. He held him in a firm grip just below his shoulders. The man was saying something but he couldn't hear – well not at first, but then slowly he began to listen.

'It's all right. Can you understand me?' said the figure in a soft, yet deep voice.

Gavin nodded his head, and then it all came flooding back to him. It was like emerging from a long, dark tunnel. He began to remember – began to *see*...

The man in front spoke again. He was dressed in a vivid red and yellow stretch lycra suit and had striking features. He was still holding on to Gavin's arms.

'You're safe now,' said the multi–coloured spectacle as he began to relax his grip.

'No!' shouted Gavin. 'Don't let g...'

The taut, stretched bungee rope snatched at Gavin's ankles. It whisked him off his feet causing him to bang his head on the varnished, planked deck of the boat where he had been stood just moments before.

The open–mouthed gathering of people gasped in horror as Gavin's screaming body hurtled away from the stern of the vessel like a missile. Wonderman looked around at the traumatized faces.

Ooops!

He shot off after Gavin using every ounce of strength from his anti–gravity flying muscles. The force of his departure was so severe, that it pushed the rear of the yacht down into the water lifting the entire forward end into the air. The effect catapulted a large number of the occupants from off the boat and into the river.

Wonderman turned his head as he heard the shrieks from below. This distracted him from his grab for Gavin ... and he missed.

Gavin hurtled up and over the bridge from where he had begun his quest. As the bungee rope stretched to its limit again, the momentum of his flight flung him back under the opposite side in a long sweeping arc. The speed at which he was travelling caused this to happen several times, wrapping him round and round. When Gavin finally came to rest, he was left suspended on the underside of the bridge, having managed to lash three newspaper photographers and a local dignitary to several parked vehicles.

Wonderman, "anti-gravved" over to the upside down – dangling – Gavin.

'*Please* don't help me anymore,' he begged, 'I have a wife and children.'

After depositing the last of the sodden passengers from the river back on board the boat, our hero apologised.

'Sorry,' he said, 'I sometimes get it wrong.'

'Oh, is that *so*...' growled a large dripping woman, then rewarded him with several blows from her waterlogged handbag. It eventually took three strong men to restrain her.

Wonderman left the scene, his head and his heart hanging very low. He didn't look back. As he disappeared over the trees and out of sight, the yacht groaned heavily and a huge crack opened up in the weakened structure. The already soaked passengers screamed again as the vessel slowly began to sink beneath the surface of the water.